ROSS GALLEN

REVOLUTION, 51ST CENTURY

REVOLUTION, 51ST CENTURY

ROSS GALLEN

Kravitz and Sons LLC
204 E Arlington Blvd. Suite B
Greenville, NC 27858

Graphics by Julie Kahles-Bhatti

Published by Kravitz and Sons LLC.

ISBN: 979-8-89639-568-3 (sc)
ISBN: 979-8-89639-569-0 (e)

Because of the dynamic nature of the Internet, any web addresses or links contained in this book may have changed since publication and may no longer be valid. The views expressed in this work are solely those of the author and do not necessarily reflect the views of the publisher, and the publisher hereby disclaims any responsibility for them.

Table of Contents

For Marj Gallen-Hanover,
Daughter of the Republic.

PROLOGUE

As most things do, the change began in an innocent manner. The country was tired and longed for change from the gotcha politics of the past twenty-five years.

A new spirit of hope abounded in the body politic regardless of the fact there was no basis in our historical development for such hope. People needed hope, something new to believe in. Something to follow that portended a better future. The spirit of the day was change.

Little attention was paid to any rational basis for change. Change was simply put out in the ether with vague promises of better times for the collective. Rational thinkers did not buy into the message of the pied piper; however the soul of the country was morally bankrupt and as any drowning man would, people held on to a toothpick in the water as if it were the flotilla of life.

It is easy to deceive, it is hard to lead. The politics of self-deception were as old as Methuselah. Attack the establishment, promise a better life and gain power. Once power is obtained crush the opposition. Appear measured and moderate in belief, tolerant of others and with the implied message that you have a better way that will bring about change for the betterment of all. That is the formula.

In practice, obtain power and drop the rubes on their head. The world of reality is different from the textbook of classroom democracy. Reality has a bite to its grip that leaves scars and gapping holes in the body. The response to reality is anger and naked aggression. Thoughtful individuals are caught in the swirling cauldron of the pestle as they are cranked through the system of bureaucratic mendacity.

Hope begins to fade and the individual simply craves the peace of sleep that accompanies the blackness of the night. Reality comes back in its own form as the sun rises on the horizon. As the world of shadows fades from the reality of the night, light shines on the countenance of the individual and a new strength emerges supplanting the dark shadows of the night.

George Bush had a vision. He wanted to bring democracy to the dark corners of the world. He believed that if you gave a man a bowl of rice and put in place a system of checks and balances to protect the rice bowl, a new way of life would emerge from the rice bowl. You could do national building from the core out that would benefit the medieval primitivism of Middle Eastern society.

He was roundly criticized for his blunt talk and simple mannerisms. The Europeans preferred to maintain the medieval societies of the Middle East for the sake of profit. In the boldest sense, 21st century Europeans were little different than their 19th century counterparts.

In the 19th century the colonials drew artificial lines in the sand and gave each country a name. No attention was paid to ethnic history or political geography. Instead the objective of the action was to empower an artificial ruling class that would subjugate the other social classes, and live a life of luxury, all the while plundering the riches of the land in the name of colonialism. It was a wonderful system that worked well for many years.

The House of Saud became wealthy and sent its sons to the finest schools in England. The desert nomad transformed from a herder of camels to a Bentley operator.

Other despots arose who lacked the social veneering of the Saudis.

The straight talking man from Texas viewed his ascendancy to power as a mandate to spread the good news of democracy. Just as the early Christians spread the good news, George Bush sought to bring the concept of democratic rule to the dark corners of the earth.

He failed to recognize that some people and societies are so exclusive and ethnocentric that there is no room for disbelief or doubt. His mission was doomed to failure because there are those in out midst for whom no amount of explanation, handholding or good will is sufficient to open their eyes to the reality of life in the 21st century.

All the while that the war in Iraq persisted there was a mean spirit of political destruction taking place. People became polarized. The center ground of the political spectrum evaporated under the blazing sun of August sky.

A schism developed in the American psyche that undercut the values of tolerance and free speech. The very soul of the nation was wrenched apart.

Once before this country had been led into war to preserve the English colonies. Woodrow Wilson characterized it as a war to save democracy. Historians saw it as a gamble to preserve the existing economic order. Through American intervention the order was preserved, but preservation sowed the seeds of the Second World War and ultimately the economic colonies of Asia and the Middle East sought their own level of governance.

The European formula prevailed, and all seemed well until 9-11.

George Bush was a visionary. He saw the world in black and white and used 9-11 as the justification to jettison the old social order. It does not matter if he was right or wrong. It is merely a fact that happened. The average American on the street had little stomach for prolonged war and his commitment to Independence Day was to barbecue hot dogs and have a cold beer. The war in Iraq and Afghanistan went on too long. America longed for change, for a new direction and new order. Sometimes you get what you pray for but with unintended results.

Chapter 1

Nuclear Fire Cracker

The trouble began in August. It was hot all over the country. Air conditioners were strained to the limit as were tempers and the electric grid.

Hassan al Aziz was a patient man. He hated the west and all that it stood for. He believed that in the fullness of time the Caliphate would be reestablished and the blue eyes would be driven from the face of the earth much as you would exterminate maggots on a carcass.

He loved the call to prayer and the sense of redemption he experienced in the mosque. His vision of life was to rid the world of the Christian infidels and their Jewish supporters.

If only God would give him a sign. His view of the world would be confusing to people raised in the West. After all, he was a merchant with a wife and family and had a piece of the pie. It was maintained that such people do not make good terrorist recruits.

Hassan was a great believer in charity; however his charity was the Muslim Brotherhood. It wasn't exactly the Salvation Army but that did not seem to bother the powers in Washington in the waning days of the Swanson administration. Everyone from the Secretary of War to the Chairman of the Joint Chief's of Staff believed that if we only engaged in dialogue with our adversaries, they would see they are just like us and everything will be nice and OK.

We needed to take into account their just demands and grievances. The same naive beliefs of Jimmy Carter that set the stage for Khomeini and his gang of thugs was being played again, but this time on a much larger scale.

The Inman called the faithful to prayer and Hassan felt the comfort of the Koran. After services a few of the faithful gathered for a political meeting.

The Inman informed Hassan that he and his family had been chosen to visit America and deliver an offering to the new Mosque that was being constructed in the heart of Los Angeles. Hassan felt greatly honored and was excited to see for himself the decadent way in which Americans lived.

He accepted the tickets and made arrangements for a passport for himself and his family to visit America. Secretly he wanted to see Disneyland. He kept it to himself. On the day before departure he stopped by the Mosque to collect the gift package for the new Mosque in Los Angeles. It was heavy and weighed almost 60 pounds. Nonetheless he promised to deliver it with great pleasure.

What Hassan did not know was that all over the Muslim world a similar scene was playing itself out. Other Hassans were picking up their packages for delivery to mosques in America.

On the day of departure, Hassan, his wife and their six children boarded the Egypt Air Flight to New York. There was an air of excitement because none of them had ever traveled on an airplane, let alone traveled out of Egypt. He clutched his beads in his hands and thanked Allah for the wonderful present bestowed on him and his family.

It was a long flight and all the children could talk about was going to "It's A Small World" when they got to Disneyland. After clearing customs in New York their flight continued on to Los Angeles.

When they were about 200 miles out, the pilot called Air Traffic Control for his final clearance. They started the descent into LAX from an altitude of 37,000 feet. When they descended to 30,000 feet the bomb went off. Hassan never knew that in this brief moment of blast and heat he would never see his children again. His world ended without comment. The blast, heat and radiation changed the face of the world.

Hassan's bomb went off with 10 others over the Los Angeles Basin. Heat and radiation was wide spread and contained within the basin. Now it was simply a basin of death.

#

Dave and Meri were ordinary Americans. They were born during the Second World War. They were ingrained with values of honesty and integrity. Early on they were taught to believe in hard work and not look to anyone for a handout or a government program to fund their way through life.

Dave remembered the first time he was really aware of Meri. They were in the seventh grade in Mrs. Squires' class. Meri was really annoying him. She sat behind him and kept kicking his chair. When he would turn around she started giggling at him. That made him madder and he did not know quite what to do. He came home from school, and his mother asked why he was so upset. Not knowing what to say, he just said, "Things."

In 1952 most families if they were fortunate had one telephone line coming into the house. The phone belonged to mom and pop. If you talked for more than a few minutes mom was standing over you demanding surrender of the telephone. Dave's house was no different. It was Friday night and his parents went out for Mexican food to La Cantena Restaurant.

He heard the phone ringing and ran from upstairs to the down stairs hallway where the telephone rested. He picked up the phone and said, "Hello." All he got in response was some giggling on the other end. Hanging up the phone he went back to his room and listened to "The Shadow" on his Silverton radio. The radio was his prized possession.

No one in the neighborhood had TV, because the sets were too expensive and the programming was still very limited. He had just sat down at his little desk when the telephone rang again. He thought to himself, "I hope this is important, because I am missing my program." When he got to the phone and picked it up, before he said anything there was the same giggling. Now he got really pissed off because someone was crank calling him. He wondered who it was because all of his friends were guys and none of them sounded like the giggling on the other end.

In the 9th grade Dave began to take notice of girls. There was one girl that really flashed through his mind every day. He could not wait to go to school and see her. He never really talked to her, but he liked to look at her. She had brown hair and green eyes and the biggest boobs he had ever seen on a little girl.

He had never really seen girl's boobs except in his Playboy magazine, but he imagined what her's looked like under her bra. She used to wear a semi transparent gossamer blouse to school and he could see the back outline of her bra. It had three hooks and he imagined himself unfastening those hooks and just looking at her skin.

Once in a while she would turn his way and they would exchange looks. In the 12th grade he finally mustered the courage to ask her to the prom. She asked him, "Why did it take so long for you to ask me out?" He did not know what to say. Men of his time were more bashful and there were more clearly defined social rules between the sexes.

The prom was the best night of his life. In his mind he remembered picking Meri up at her parents home. He brought her a corsage made of pink orchids. He would never forget the picture she made as she walked down the winding staircase to the hallway of her parents home. She was dressed in a tight fitting navy blue satin gown. Her hair was pulled up in a French braid and he could see highlights of gold color contrasted against the deep chestnut brown of her real hair color. She was the most beautiful thing he had ever seen in his life.

After prom night they decided to go to college together. Meri had worked as a candy striper at the county hospital and wanted to be a nurse. Dave's father was a lawyer and he thought he would follow in his foot steps.

Meri finished school and came back to Las Vegas to work at University Medical Center. She missed not being able to see Dave every day but he was studying hard. Law school was very tough. One of the instructors said, "Look to the right, now look to your left. That person will not be here at the beginning of the new term." The attrition rate was terrible. More than 50% of the first year students flunked out. It was not because they were not smart. Smarts was only part of the issue. You had to be a grind. It was not like college where you could cram at the last minute and ace the test. Law school tested the person's whole sum of knowledge. There was no place for laggards.

The theory was that if you represented a client whose life or money was at stake, he was entitled to 300% of what you were. Nothing more and nothing less. If you were not prepared to give it, then you did not belong in the profession.

There is a saying in law school. The first year they scare you to death, the second year they work you to death and the third year they bore you to death. Dave was now in his third year of law school and Meri was beginning to wonder where she really fit into his life. It felt like he was married to the law and that not much else was important to him. Their weekends together became explosive and she finally put it to him.

"I want to know where we are going with this relationship. I don't have the next ten years for you to find yourself!"

Dave seemed startled by her remarks and exclaimed, "Look Meri, I still have the bar examination ahead of me and then I have to find a job, and I don't have any money. I can't marry you and ask my parents to support us."

Meri was waiting for this. She had given a lot of thought to what she was about to say.

"David Marston, I am going to support you for the next two years. I have a good job and you can move into my place. You study and pass the bar and when you finish you're going to pull the family wagon."

Meri was full of fire. It never ceased to amaze Dave how tough she was. Nothing bothered her. She was unfazed.

When they started their life together Vegas was a small town. There was an old Mormon establishment in town that seemed to be doing well through hard work and good social networking. Meri and Dave did not belong to any church. They just believed in live and let live.

Systemic changes were taking place and new people were moving in from all over. There was opportunity for plain folk to make a living in the many casinos that had sprung up. Dave ended up opening a small private practice doing criminal defense and family law. He saw a good slice of life. He enjoyed criminal defense practice because the pendulum was swinging in favor of upholding the rights of the individual in defiance of the state's arbitrary abridgement of civil rights. He in fact became a journeyman at his profession and always stood up to those who would abridge or take shortcuts with basic human rights and liberties.

Meri worked on and off at UMC as the mood struck her. There was always a shortage of skilled nurses. The hospital had its large cadre of nurses from the Philippines, but they were culturally distinguishable from the American mainstream and some of the patients would treat them as if they were uneducated foreigners.

That always annoyed Meri because while their English and mannerism may have been a little difficult to understand, their commitment to care was genuine and Meri would never permit anyone to exhibit overt prejudice in her presence.

Dave made a lot of money, but the money never seemed very important to him. His idea of a good time was letting Meri make him laugh. She had a wonderful way of putting him in his place. He even forgave her for the crank calls when they were in junior high school. They had a wonderful life together.

#

In Islamabad there was a small mosque where the resident Inman was preaching against the sins of the flesh and the evils of the West. In particular his sermon of the day railed against the fleshpot of evil in Las Vegas. "They and all of their kind must burn in the fires of hell for all eternity. Allah akba, Allah akba!"

#

Dave and Meri were sitting in their living room with granddaughter Amy when the nukes went off. The entire Las Vegas Valley was incinerated. Their universe ceased to exist. Hell had come to Las Vegas.

#

In other parts of the United States the situation repeated itself. There was widespread death and destruction. The President and his staff were quickly taken aboard Air Force One and the retaliation was swift and without mercy.

It was of little consolation to those who lost their loved ones and family. Patriotism is only meaningful if you are alive and able to participate in the act.

The intellectually empty pacification program that began with Jimmy Carter and culminated with Swanson had come to its inevitable conclusion. Three hundred million people died because the Ayatollahs and their supporters in the Muslim Brotherhood were not just like us. They did not want to sit down and reason together. They viewed us as weak and corrupt and spat upon our women and institutions.

We lacked their ability to have a direct pipeline to God, and all those people paid for it with their lives.

The breakup of the Soviet Union provided the opportunity for the Muslim Brotherhood to acquire the Russian Suitcase Nukes. The death of three hundred million Americans caused a reevaluation of where we were going as a society. Fundamental change was necessary, and even it would not preserve the American way of life. The nature of the change required us to trash many of our values.

Chapter 2

Gaul

As a child Gaul always knew he was different from the other boys. He looked like the others; five fingers, five toes, grey eyes and olive colored skin, but he sensed some difference. As a child he was quiet and not prone to gregarious behavior. He always felt it was best to be self-controlled and not display his inner self.

He questioned mentally whether other boys were the same, but never in a verbal context. His thoughts remained his own.

He began to develop two distinct personalities. There was the outer mask that he displayed in public, and the inner person that only he knew. He longed to be able to talk to someone about his inner thoughts and questions but instinctively realized it would be dangerous to reveal himself.

As he grew into his teens he was required to take an adolescent matriculation examination to measure his potential academic and physical skills for the purpose of determining how best he could serve the Secretariat. This was a normal right of passage that all boys went through and was in effect the gateway to manhood. Even though the state had long before embarked on a program of selective breeding the matriculation examination was the gateway to further development within the hierarchy of the state.

A bad grade or mere passing score on the matriculation exam would relegate him to the Combat Infantry Legion and twenty years of hard service. Few survived the hard conditions and grueling conditions of life found in the Combat Infantry Legion. It was not a place that anyone wanted to end up. You did not rise in the ranks and become an officer. What was expected was absolute obedience to authority and a complete willingness to sacrifice yourself for the good of the state.

Of course there were rewards. Money had long ceased to be a medium of exchange. Personal satisfaction came in the form of sexual satisfaction regardless of personal aberration or depravity. It was OK and sanctioned doing what ever felt good. Sex in a sense became a method of control. Food and spirits were always available in excellent quality and quantity. This was in keeping with the genetic advances made in agriculture.

Education and knowledge for the Legion were limited to instruction in military doctrine and the use of arms in offensive operations. There was no Uniform Code of Military Justice because the concept of the enemy as a human being did not exist. The concept had been eliminated from the English language. There was them and there was us. Combat was to the death and prisoners were never taken. The motto of the unit was to come home victorious or come home dead. There was no in between. When the enemy surrendered, he was interrogated and summarily executed. Mercy was a concept that did not exist. After all what would we do with fifty enemy prisoners? The thought of detaining them in camps and feeding them made no sense. The thought of re-education and resettlement was equally untenable. These concepts never occurred to members of the Combat Infantry Legion. Everything was to the death. If you were lucky enough to last 20 years of combat duty you were retired to South Padre Island in Texas. I do not know why they picked this spot, but perhaps it was because of the relative isolation from the remainder of New America.

For women, those who did not make the grade became the concubines of the Combat Infantry Legion. It was not really clear what the standards were for a woman to pass the matriculation examination. Women of this grade were treated as sex slaves to do the bidding of the Legion. They existed in camps where Legionnaires came for rest and recreation. Their sole function was to satisfy the cravings of Legionnaires. Sometimes there were terrible physical abuses of the women, but these abuses were looked at with a jaundiced eye because after all the security of the state is what counted the most, and life was pledged to the Secretariat. There was a high rate of suicide among the women, but they were quickly replaced with younger models.

Breeding as a matter of procreation between a man and a woman had ceased. At best it was a primitive means of selection of the next generation. After the great day of destruction it was necessary to quickly marshal the resources of the country and create an army of men that could defend what was left of old America. The President turned to his scientists for a solution. The solution was obvious but it took several years to put into place the technology for extra womb production of infants. The President exerted great leadership skills and the nation's scientists turned inward as if to excise a cancerous problem. So many Americans had radiation damage to their genetic code. It was necessary to find men and women who were free of damage and quickly replicate from their genes. It was in fact a matter of national survival.

The first 50 years were very shaky. There were a lot of duds. There were ethical issues involved with breeding people to perpetuate the human race. Many of the old people who held strong religious persuasions felt that breeding of this kind did not distinguish us from the animals of the farm or creatures of the forest. They argued that God had implanted man with a soul and that since man was created in the image of God this was a sacrilegious desecration of the worst magnitude. Others took a more pragmatic position. They adopted the notion that species survival is what counts and that God was merely a fiction that was adopted by primitive man to explain the universe when primitive man lacked understanding of fire and the basic laws of physics. Eventually the religious people died out and with their disappearance their ideas summarily died.

This was the world that Gaul was born into. Language is a funny thing. If you talk to a primitive man and ask him how many deer he saw in the forest, he will tell you one, two or many. The number 3 does not exist in his lexicon. So it was with God, and the human soul. They ceased to exist because there was no necessity for them or verbal reference to them.

Chapter 3

Gaul

Thinking back to his childhood in the Kinder Haus it suddenly dawned on Gaul that he never had a father or mother. The words did not exist in his lexicon. The Secretariat was his parent.

In the Old Testament the word for mother was Emma. In English the word became mother. In the origin of the Hebrew people Rachel was the mother of all Jews. Now the mother of all was the Secretariat. It was the Secretariat that trained the technicians and maintained the kinder hospitals where children were born. One never knew a father or mother, but a person's DNA pattern was a matter of government record, open to those who had the need to know.

Gaul's origin was a mixture of farmed DNA patterns that were designed to create the next generation of man. The technicians were not completely clear on their objectives and breeding standards. It was necessary to closely monitor them to be certain they acted in the best interest of the Secretariat.

Trust was not a commodity that was easy to imply in the character of those who worked in this most sensitive area. There was always suspicion and doubt. The Secretariat kept matters under control to the highest degree possible. There could always be a traitor in the midst of the operation and there was no escape from the need to remain vigilant.

The problem with the kinder hospitals was that humans were so long lived, 150 years long and therefore it took a long time to see if the desired genetic patterns and traits were developing in accordance with the standards desired by the Secretariat. With dogs and mice it was easy to breed desired outward characteristics because of their short life spans. Generational issues quickly revealed themselves.

With men and women there was no such quick unveiling. It could take over a hundred years of observation to know what you had developed.

Gaul was amused by the matriculation examination. He was physically in the top percentile for his species. On the mental side of matters he displayed a high facility with language. His language facility was of particular interest to the Committee.

He had been brought to the attention of the Committee at an early age by his proctors. There were those on the Committee who openly favored his further development in the belief that he would ultimately compete for a place at the Secretariat, and those who feared him because of his mental prowess and wished him eliminated.

Gaul was unaware of their thoughts and findings as he completed the examination. His real inner self was drifting far away to another place and time. In the course of preparing for the matriculation examination, Gaul had come across strange phenomena that he was afraid to mention to anyone. He and his friend were on the west coast of what was old America and decided to drop down into what had been Las Vegas. Even in the culture of the day there was a memory of Las Vegas as the entertainment center of the world. He wanted to see for himself what was left of the place.

The radioactivity had ceased to be a problem, but the ruins were everywhere. The air car dropped down from an altitude of 40,000 feet and he could see the whole Las Vegas Valley and what was left of the city and its adjoining environments. There was really not a lot to see, save for broken piece of concrete here and there, and desert vegetation slowly creeping in and overtaking the entire valley. Gaul urged his friend to drop lower and then to land their craft. It was as if something was drawing him to the old city.

As they approached the ground, a giant dust cloud began to swirl around them. Sand and debris were thrown in every direction. As the air car touched down he could see an old street sign that said Las Vegas Blvd 800. The dryness and lack of rainfall had preserved the sign for over 3,000 years. The paint on the sign had long since weathered away but the bare metal was clearly discernable. Gaul felt a sense of excitement and exhilaration pass through him.

He had a premonition that he was about to make a discovery that would change the course of his life. Little did he understand what was about to happen.

"Charlie, let's go see what we can find."

Charlie looked around and all he could see was sand and debris.

"I don't like this place. It gives me the creeps. Beside, everyone who ever lived here is dead. What do you think we are going to find? I want to get out of here."

Gaul was not one to be easily deterred. He quickly moved forward and looked in every direction from the sign. Silently he thought to himself, "I wonder what was here?" He had no way to know that just a short distance away buried beneath the sand was the Las Vegas Public Library. Of course he did not know what a Public Library was, because in his time there was no public repository for books and ideas. Everyone had a computer terminal, entry code and screen and all necessary information came from it. The notion of a Library where there were books with multiple viewpoints and ideas was not within his thought process.

Gaul realized that any further discussion with Charlie was pointless and that if he was really interested in this place he would have to return on his own.

Chapter 4

Gaul

Five grueling years passed before Gaul would find his way back to the sign at Las Vegas Boulevard. He did not know why but the sign was always there in his mind beckoning him to return. At times he would wake up in the dark hours of the night and see it flash before him. All he could do was to wonder what lay beneath the sign. After a time it became an obsession to discover what was there.

As fate would have it he was selected to become an officer in the Combat Infantry Legion. He was uncertain why he had been selected because he had a wide range of interests, the least of which was killing people.

He recognized that it took a cold mentality to consciously take the life of another person who has not personally invaded his space. The Legion would do all that was possible to change his thinking.

Leadership was based on adherence to objective and the ability to command with absolute obedience. Gaul had problems with the leadership concept. While he accepted adherence to objective as a necessary component of leadership, he questioned the ability to command with absolute obedience. In his mind the two were irreconcilable concepts.

Then again there was a distinct division between the officer core and foot sloggers of the Legion. They appeared to know their place and had no such doubts as he experienced. They swore their oath of allegiance to the Secretariat and that is what they accepted and believed.

Gaul was uncertain if other officers were plagued by his doubts, but kept his thoughts to himself. He began to experience the fear that comes with exploration and uncertainty of one's place in the scheme of life. Exposure can be very dangerous if you cannot place your fate in the hands of your fellows. It was a problem that gnawed away at the core of his existence.

If Gaul had a father or a mother in whom to confide or to mimic as a role model he would not have been so troubled. All that he had was his memory of life in the Kinder Haus and the competition to rise to the top. Sometimes he found himself confused by the order of battle. Left to their own, the foot sloggers were incapable of assuming command or making rational operational decisions. They were dependent on the officers to lead them in the order of battle.

Gaul saw the obvious shortcomings of the system. It amused him. He wondered why this differentiation had taken place. Obviously it was genetic in origin because the breeding pools were controlled by the state, and the laboratories created units that were considered desirable by the Secretariat.

In giving it more consideration, Gaul wondered if the genetic technicians simply lacked the ability to uniformly breed bright units. If that were the case there would always be an endless supply of foot sloggers. The thoughts coursed through his mind. He understood that such thoughts were heresy and that if he openly voiced them trouble would quickly follow. He amused himself by constantly examining the concept and seeking logical conclusions. None came.

He was now a squad leader of 100 Legionnaires. It was not a difficult position but simply one that he had to pass through on his move to the top. He understood his conduct was being observed and everything he did was being noted in his file. The trick was not to end up in the Blue File of the area commander. That would be the end of his career and would ultimately relegate him to a minor position. He knew what he had to do.

It occurred to him that the best commander does not lead by giving orders but by saying, "Follow Me." A commander must be fearless of his own demise and must set the standard for everyone else. Gaul resolved to be that person. His resolve became ingrained in his psyche.

It was August and they were training for a mission in Iraq. Three thousand years later we were still fighting in Iraq. What better place to train then the Las Vegas Valley. It had low levels of radiation with some hot pockets of radioactivity. August was hot with dry winds coming off the coast of Baja, California. There was an occasional thunderstorm. It mimicked the conditions they would find in Iraq. All that was missing were the Afghan Hodgies.

It was a good test of their equipment and combat readiness. Gaul wondered how his platoon would hold up under the harsh desert conditions. The Legion was not like armies of old that practiced with paint guns and simulated mockups of enemy towns. Everything in the Legion was tailored to reality. Live fire exercise was the order of the day.

The doctrine was that the survivors would be the better soldiers and more competent to inflict losses on the enemy. Warfare had changed. Men on white horses did not lead charges. Wounds were no longer fixable. Bullets did not pass through soldiers and simply rip out chunks of flesh and bone that could be repaired.

The standard issue infantry weapon was a Remington Blast Rifle. It was a particularly nasty weapon. At 2000 yards it fired a beam of energy that ripped through the vital organs of the recipient. Wounds were so catastrophic that medical corpsman ceased to be an element of the battlefield. A seriously wounded Legionnaire knew his time was over and simply accepted his fate.

Today it was the Reds against the Blues. Gaul did not intend to lose.

"Sergeant Cross, I want you to set up two encampments on the high ground of the south Las Vegas Valley." Cross implicitly understood his orders. He was pleased to serve a zealous commander because it insured his own survival.

"Sergeant Major, I also want you to calculate the effective range of the blast rifles and create a cross-fire killing zone." Cross already knew the effective range of the blast rifles and nodded his compliance.

Turning to his squad leader he ordered 75 Legionnaires to set up an open encampment at the base of the valley, with little security.

The men on the slopes dug in and hydrated.

Gaul was prepared to wait for as long as it would take for the Blue Team to come in. He knew he was sacrificing the lives of 75 Legionnaires for his own survival and advancement. The thought did not bother him. They were expendable, much as the brass from an old rifle was left behind without an afterthought. The 75 men made a soft target.

The Blue Team was led by Roscoe Davis. He was an impulsive young man who fancied himself in the style of Custer. His scouts reconnoitered the Red Team Camp. He questioned them closely. "What did you find?"

The lead scout replied, "Sir, the Red Team's encampment appears to be lightly defended. It is not operating in a defensive position in accord with sound military doctrine."

Roscoe Davis was a suspicious man. He knew better than to trust the observation of a simple Legionnaire scout. He ordered up two drones with night flying visibility and personally observed the ground as they hovered at high altitude hidden from ground view. The drones confirmed the observation of the Legionnaires. As the sun rose in the morning he ordered the attack on the Red Team Camp. The Red Team was totally unprepared. There was no leadership. The sun was in their eyes. In 30 minutes their corpses littered the floor of the valley at the base of the south rim of the mountain.

Body parts were loosely scattered about the volcanic rock. In most cases it was impossible to distinguish which arm belonged to a particular torso. The Blue Team slowly moved in and looked for any stragglers. None were found. Blue Team suffered no causalities.

Roscoe was feeling very confident. He was on his way up. He was confident of his total victory.

"Sergeant, I want you to collect the body parts and burn them."

"Sir, what about a head count?"

"No need to worry sergeant, we eliminated the whole Red Team."

Military planning is about preparation, more preparation, rehearsal and good intelligence. His victory was so swift that it never occurred to him to double check by counting the dead. More importantly it did not occur to him that the Blue Team leader would knowingly sacrifice 75 Legionnaires for the purpose of creating an ambush.

Roscoe Davis was shrewd and aggressive but lacked the cold detachment that was necessary for command. As the bodies burned Blue Team set up its own encampment knowing that it would be seven days before they were extracted from the area.

During the first day sentries were set up. They walked, looked and listened. There was no sound to be heard. The second day was a repeat of the first. The third day was particularly hot. The temperature hit 120 degrees. Discipline started to fall apart. Roscoe knew that he had to let up on the men. There was no reason to maintain strict order and beside that the enemy was dead.

On the fifth day, the troop looked like an encampment of weekend hikers. Soldiers always seem to know where to find alcohol. Blue group was no different. Perhaps they brought it with them because there were no stop and go stores in the desert. Beer and drugs appeared from no where and discipline fell apart. Nighttime came. The moon was obscured by high cloud cover.

Gaul and his men emerged from their underground holes. Their faces and bodies were covered by black volcanic dust. Their bodies were cramped from the days of confinement in the ground. They smelled of feces and urine. The night air felt cool and good to taste.

"Sergeant Major, I want 5 men to get behind their camp and place these incendiary bombs. We are going to light up the night sky behind them so that their every move is visible. As soon as these bombs go off they are going to run in every direction. They won't be able to run away. If anyone tries to get behind the fire, kill them! Otherwise hold your fire and maintain your silence. We will do the rest."

The Legionnaires standing around Gaul did not question him. They knew the remainder of his orders would be forthcoming.

"I want 10 Legionnaires on each side of the rim. When the fires go off, you shoot anything that moves. If you have any doubts shoot again. Do not try to save on ammunition. Everyone check to make certain that you have three sets of energy spares. I will not permit any survivor from Red Group. If you take any prisoners execute them!"

The incendiaries went off and confusion reigned just as Gaul had predicted. The Legionnaires shot straight. In ten minutes it was over. The entire Blue Team was dead. Gaul congratulated himself on a mission accomplished. In two days they would be extricated. Gaul now had the opportunity to check out the sign.

Chapter 5

Gaul

Gaul tossed in the night in a troubled sleep. He was not concerned about the loss of three quarters of his platoon or the deaths of the entire Blue Team. This was what he had trained for. Rather something else was bothering him that he could not quite pinpoint. He had the feeling that something was missing from his life. His concept did not extend out to all life because he was a product of his environment which made it clear that at most the universe was limited to one long life span of no more than 150 years. Yet there was something missing. Perhaps that is the nature of man, to question and to seek.

Primitive man hovered in his cave and was afraid of lightening. He treated the fire from the sky as a negative message from the Gods. In Gaul's world there was no God, there was no fear, there was only the inevitable end of life and the closing of one's personal universe. It was indeed a dark world.

Gaul told his troops to take a break for the next two days until evac time when they would be picked up.

"I don't want any heavy drinking or drug use, and everybody goes home.

You got it?"

There was a small choir of voices that acknowledged his order.

"Yes sur- thank you sir."

With that he turned on the group, and began to assemble a kit with water for two days and a small titanium shovel. He took some light explosive charges with him, and of course his Remington in the event he encountered something out of the ordinary.

"Sergeant Major, you're in charge. I expect to be back in two days and find everything in its place. Do you understand?"

Sergeant Major Drummy looked at him out of the corner of his eye and nodded. He knew better than to question an officer and especially one as ruthless as Gaul. He would do what it took to keep the Legionnaires in line.

Gaul's departure was unceremonious. He figured that walking all through the night he could make the 12 clicks to the sign by daybreak. Walking during the day was not an option in the August heat.

Gaul silently proceeded down the remains of what used to be I-15. The asphalt was broken. The desert had reclaimed much of the road, but even after all this time it was distinctly visible to the naked eye. When he got to St. Rose Parkway he decided to shift over to the east and intersect Las Vegas Boulevard off of St. Rose. There was less damage to the road by taking this direction and he felt it would be easier to travel the necessary distance.

He stopped to drink and to pee. His urine was a curious dark yellow indicative that something was going wrong with his body function. The toll of the week had compromised his body functions. He knew that his time on location would be short and that he did not have the energy to sustain a prolonged stay. Beside that who would come back for him in the event he failed to return? Gaul was confident that he would simply be written off as a casualty of the exercise. Such was the way of the world.

As he approached the area where he remembered the street sign, it was still there. It appeared to be undisturbed. A silent sentry standing in testimony to the past. Gaul pulled the mine detector out of his bottom pant pocket. Miniaturization had come a long way in 3,000 years, but the object was still the same. The key was to find the metal object. Turning it on he thought it might come in handy in locating something below.

As he walked up the street, the red diode began to blink in a furious manner. It was as if someone were beckoning to him to come to a specific place. Finally the diode stopped blinking and simply remained red. He found himself standing up against what must have been a wall. Closer examination revealed that it was actually an aluminum door with a glass insert that had been covered over by 3,000 years of sand and dust. He had no idea how the door mechanism operated. The ready solution was to take a small amount of explosive and blow an entry way into the location. He did so.

Walking through the building was a wondrous experience. There appeared to be books, many books on shelves scattered throughout the floor. He did not understand what the purpose of the room was. Eventually he came to what appeared to be a soundproofed room. Inspecting its contents he saw what looked like headsets. They were primitive by comparison to today's standards but their purpose was obvious. He thought, "What is it that people listened to?" Turning to his right he spotted a primitive CD. It was so large. Again technology had advanced in the last 3,000 years. Looking around he sought a player for the CD. It then occurred to him that even if he found the player there was no electricity to run it.

The CD player was very rudimentary. He jury rigged the power from his personal light to the CD player. When he inserted the CD he fully expected to hear a voice of some kind with a recorded message. Instead what he heard was the opening movement of Beethoven's 9th Symphony.

He was spellbound. This was the first time in his life that he heard music. Music as a source of esthetic pleasure had disappeared shortly after the outbreak of the Great War. Musical instruments were discarded in favor of the practical necessities it took to maintain a country that was for the most part destroyed when the nuclear genie was let out of the bottle.

Gaul sat transfixed in the rapture of the sound. When the final movement came about he recognized the sound of human voices in great harmony, but not the language. He wondered, "Was there another language beside basic English or Arabic? What is it that is being said?" His world began to spin out of control. He began to question all of the assumptions that were spoon fed to him. Picking up the jacket of the CD, Gaul read Schiller's "Ode to Joy."

He knew he had stumbled upon something that he craved in the inner recess of his soul. Thinking over Schiller's words he wondered how all men could be brothers. How can one have a father? He knew he must keep this secret to himself. To reveal it was to risk certain death.

Chapter 6

Children's Games

Gaul had never really considered what it was like to have a mother and father. Having grown up in the Kinder Haus such a concept was foreign to him. He could not conceive how anyone could love a child without reservation, simply because it was a child of the body. Such a concept was alien to him. After all, children were units to serve the greater good of the Secretariat.

He began to spend all of his free time excising the vast resources of the Library. With great curiosity he watched family films of the mid 20th century. He was amazed that the nuclear family formed the basic building block of the national consciousness, and that children were venerated for themselves regardless of their utility to the state. This conception of family was completely at odds with all that he had been taught. It was anathema to his life experience. He wondered if there was some kernel of truth that would reveal itself from the existence of the family unit.

Sitting at his terminal it occurred to him that he had to explore for himself the notion that families as opposed to Kinder Haus should raise children. He was stunned by the concept that his personal cultural memories and values independent of his genetic pattern could live on in his descendants. What a unique idea. A dangerous one because if implemented it would shake the foundations of the Secretariat to the core. It was an idea that was directly contrary to the values that had been instilled in him. In the most fundamental sense it represented the Great Heresy.

How does one engage in a mission of exploration where the very thought of exploration is a challenge to the existing social order such that the sanction is death. It was a troubling consideration. Gaul knew he had to visit the primary genetic engineering lab in Capital City to observe for himself whether his thoughts were mere folly or if there was some specific substance to them. Capital City was the nerve center of the country. Here the great labs existed along with the great thinkers and scientists of the time. He chose to spend his time at the Central Bionics Lab.

He entered the lab in full uniform. The receptionist was taken aback because she had never seen a Colonel General of the Legion up close. He was much younger then she would have expected. She instantly decided to ingratiate herself to him.

"How can I help you?"

"I want to see the Director. Tell him that General Gaul requests a few moments of his time, and that I would be most appreciative if he could accommodate me."

She turned to her side and spoke into a hidden intercom. In a few moments the Director emerged from a side panel. There was a huge smile on his face. The director knew that Gaul was not someone he wanted to offend. For that matter he did not want Gaul to know that he even existed. Better to maintain his anonymity. However in the face of what might be a crisis, he knew that he should smile his way through the maze.

"General Gaul, what a pleasure! What can I do for you?"

Gaul took the full measure of the man. The Director did not give the appearance of an academic type. He was a manager, adept at the infighting of the bureaucracy. A man who would sell his soul and his friends for personal advancement. There appeared to be a perpetual smile on his face that masked the hidden man. Gaul had seen many men like this in the past. They filled the swank restaurants and cultural events of Capital City. This was a dangerous man who could be counted on to look out for himself and no one else.

"I want to see the laboratory where genetic processing of humans takes place."

The Directors eyes began to squint. He wondered if this was some kind of undercover investigation or a prelude to charges of ineptness in management of the Central Bionics Lab. In his mind he quickly reviewed the massive experiment that had gone wrong a few days ago, and then concluded that Gaul could not have gotten wind of it as of yet. No, this was probably just a generic visit to satisfy idle curiosity. He began to relax and breathed a sigh of relief.

"Yes, yes, of course I will be glad to give you a personal tour of the entire facility."

As they walked deeper into the module Gaul looked around at the cold walls that encased the facility. They had a sterile gray appearance. He could not help but feel that time stood still within the confines of the facility.

"I don't understand how this facility works. I mean I know that human DNA comes in here, gets recombined and units are produced but I don't really understand the assumptions."

This was going to be easier than he thought; all he had to do was answer a few questions, show the General around and he was out of his hair.

The Director was no scientist but he had heard the explanation of the Institute's work explained so many times that he could parrot the words such that they seemed to be coming from a knowledgeable research scientist.

"Well, you see here is how it works. At the end of the Great War we knew that the germ plasma of most of the population was damaged beyond repair. The country was dying. Something had to be done to quickly maintain continuity. We knew that DNA has a shape like a corkscrew ladder. There are many rungs on the ladder. The information on what constitutes a man is contained in each one of those rungs on the ladder. We developed a technique to salvage desirable rungs from the survivors of the Great War. Different people had varying parts of their genetic code that was useful. An arbitrary determination was made as to what constituted desirable genetic material. There were two primary considerations. First was intelligence and second was health. The reverse of the order makes no difference. Because of the limited number of survivors racial considerations were eliminated as a selection criteria. A technique was developed to splice the desirable genes into the ladder. The most critical part of the puzzle was to reproduce units in as fast a manner as was possible. Biotechnical engineers working in conjunction with mechanical engineers and super computers developed the artificial womb. Rather than hit or miss with pregnancies a whole generation could be created. That is what occurred."

The director seemed quite please with his explanation. It was almost as if he had done the work himself. Gaul starred back at him. Of course he had heard this explanation before. The explanation was not the real purpose of his visit.

"Tell me something, even with your gene splicing and mechanical placement of genes on the rungs of the ladder, are their failures?"

A pained look came over the Director. It was as if someone had stabbed him in the heart with a sharp knife.

"Of course there are always a certain amount of failures. No one ever said the technique was perfect. The truth is that even though we can control reproduction, the results follow the bell curve as far as the distribution of intelligence and motor skills are involved. Depending on the needs of the Secretariat and where you want to draw the line there can be upwards of 30 to 45 percent of the children who do not qualify for any kind of citizenship."

Gaul heard the words and began to shudder inside. He was almost afraid to ask the next question, but knew that he must if he was to proceed.

"And the units who fall into the low end of the bell curve, what do you do with them?"

He purposely refrained from using the word children.

The mood of the Director began to change.

"Well, what can we do with them? We have to dispose of them because after all they are of no use to the Secretariat. They are essentially property of the Secretariat."

He knew he had said too much. His choice of words was wrong. Damn, why did he have to come to work today? This crap could have come up on someone else's watch. Instead it was being laid at his feet. His day was turning to shit and he saw no improvement on the horizon. Sometimes it just doesn't pay to come to work. He was not ashamed of anything he did in his capacity as Director, but in the back of his mind there was always a lingering doubt that he was unable to articulate.

"Well, we dispose of them."

"What does that mean? Let's put all the cards on the table!"

He knew he had to carefully choose his words.

"Even with modern medicine we have older citizens whose body parts are wearing out. If we have enough time we can grow the necessary part and take prophylactic action to preserve life. Sometimes it is not possible. The defective units represent a valuable resource of body parts that can be harvested for the good of useful and productive members of the state. We simply euthanize them, and discard the carcass."

"And the others who are not used for parts replacement, what happens to them?"

"We take them apart and try to improve our splicing technique. They are an invaluable source of information. Nothing is wasted."

Gaul felt sick to his stomach. He could not believe that even in this callous age children were harvested for their body parts and dissected for the purpose of improving genetic splicing.

"What happens after you examine the genetic material?"

"It's really quite efficient, we burn the bodies, and they take up no space. We cannot afford to have them take up space. Space is at a premium."

Gaul thanked the director and exited the laboratory. The necessity for revolution was clearer in his mind.

Chapter 7

Maribeth Cooper

As an adult Maribeth Cooper was a quiet woman. She was of average appearance and build. She did not engage in wild sexual adventures and for the most part lived a solitary life. As time went on she paid little attention to her outward appearance other than to be clean. She wore no make up and dressed in simple fashion. She made a concerted effort to make herself indistinguishable from other women of her age. The effort differentiated her, but she never viewed herself in an objective manner in the mirror of life.

She lived a life of quiet obscurity, far from the peering eyes of the Secretariat. As a child she had always asked, why? Why was this and why was that? Her questions were always met with anger and resistance.

In the 7th grade the Kinder Haus school master called her in to his office.

"I have nothing but complaints about you."

Holding up a stack of papers he pushed them into her face. She began to tremble. She could feel tears coming to her eyes. She fought to control herself.

"Perhaps you are defective and don't belong here? I don't know what to do with you. You ask too many questions. Only defectives ask so many questions because they are too stupid to absorb the rules."

Hearing the word "defective" struck fear in her body. She knew that defectives were harvested for body parts. Those that didn't contain salvageable parts were quickly disposed of. She was acutely conscious of death at a tender age. It struck absolute panic in her mind. Were they going to harvest her heart or liver for someone else? Would she simply end up on the ash dump like the other defectives?

The school master went on. "Children should be seen and not heard. You do not question your teachers in the Kinder Haus. Questioning is unproductive and antisocial! With so many questions someone might think you are genetically defective. You know what that means."

On hearing "defective" again she began to twist in her seat. She could feel the hot urine dripping down her leg. She would obey.

Maribeth preserved and continued to ask questions, although not in as blunt a manner as before. She learned discretion.

When she finished the 10th grade of high school, she was diverted to the academic track for further education. She had finally learned to mask her questions and simply keep her inquiring mind to herself.

She was eventually assigned to a technical institute and trained as an IT technician for the cataloguing of state secrets. Her security clearance did not match her job title. She was ever fearful and worked hard at her job. She sought to avoid any attention from her colleagues. Finally she became a speck on the wallpaper. In cataloguing state secrets it was necessary to read and understand the documents she was keeping from public view. With every document she read she continued to ask, "Why?"

Her inquiring mind grew restless under the oppressive rule of the Secretariat.

Chapter 8

Children's Games 2

Gaul returned to his quarters. He was now a troubled man. He had moved from the top of the establishment to a provisional revolutionary. He was angry and wanted to lash out at what he perceived as a fundamental injustice.

If life were just the flip of a coin and the primary determinate was where you ended up on the gene ladder that somehow seemed wrong to him. Perhaps he had begun to internalize an idealistic view of what a family should be.

Conversely he recognized that if the State is the family and the Secretariat is the mother, some protection must be afforded to the young and defenseless. It seemed to him that merely breeding people as units imposed some further moral obligation to ensure the welfare of the unit or at least a level playing field where there was an equal opportunity for pleasure and pain.

He grappled with this conundrum for some time. He could not resolve it in his mind.

Were people really better off when raised in a family setting or when raised in the Kinder Haus? There was no clear cut set of rules. His background as a military man caused him to seek clearly defined answers where there was no room for doubt. In this case doubt pervaded his mind and there was no safe corner to retreat to.

In the idealic home of the middle class of the 18th Century, children were shielded from the aggressiveness and brutality of the outside world. The father might be off working in a factory, but the mother was there to protect her brood. The child had a value independent of the value of his body parts. In theory a child was not reducible to the value of salvageable body parts.

He had no illusion that the child or for that matter any adult had a soul or was made in the image of God. That was a convention he did not subscribe to. He viewed it as a primitive convention that served its purpose as long as man existed in the moral dimension of the Stone Age. With the advent of technology it was no longer necessary to ascribe supernatural power to unseen beings that may or may not have a beneficent view of mankind. Such was his belief be it right or wrong.

At the same time he maintained the view that whoever shared the gene type of homo sapiens climbed down out of the trees at the same time as his ancestors and that this common affinity had to be the basis of any type of comaradie between men. To his way of thinking the shared genetic code and common evolutionary experience made common ground among men, such that he became his brother's keeper. That was his conclusion.

Chapter 9

Jocelyn 5001

Jocelyn thought to herself, I like being a woman! The feeling of silk on my body is sensuous. The sensation of my bra as it tightens around my breasts makes me feel as if I am being held together by warm hands. I can feel my butt spread out as I sit on the chair in anticipation of my next sexual encounter.

Sexuality was now a matter of personal satisfaction. It had nothing to do with breeding children. Carrying someone inside of her was a ghastly thought. Breeding was best left to the homo factory farms where proper genetic material could be selected and inserted into the embryo to create useful societal units.

She had another 20 minutes before Leslie picked her up. Turning her attention to the wall monitor, she could see the new class of cadets taking their commissioning oath. She pictured herself in the same class some 10 years earlier. Not much appeared to have changed. The black and grey striped uniforms appeared to be the same. The hall with its pink granite walls appeared the same as in her memory. Why should things change, after all life is merely a wheel?

Crossing her legs she felt a certain tiredness creeping into her. Her mind was blank from the activities of the day. Her body reacted in tandem with her mind. Looking again at the monitor, the people all had a certain likeness.

It's as if they were made from the same bolt of cloth. For a moment she wondered if using replicated genes eventually produces a quotient that is no longer viable.

She watched as Secretary Warden was in the process of concluding her address. Her words had a rehearsed quality that flowed effortlessly across the crowded stadium.

"We must remember that our revolution was made to preserve our time honored laws and moral obligations. It forms the fabric that secures our law and liberty. We hand down our cherished traditions from generation to generation, taking care to inoculate each succeeding generation with the love of good order and inheritance that comes from our forefathers. We do not fear God, and look up with awe to our leadership and with reverence to the ministers and officers of government that uphold our cherished land. The universal truth of life is that our good order and the rules on which its rests are the fabric of society. I ask of each of you to take the oath of allegiance and repeat after me the following:

"I swear I will be faithful and obedient to the Secretary, that I shall render unconditional obedience to the Secretary, and that I shall at all times be ready, as a brave soldier to give my life for this oath."

The years were beginning to show on her persona. There must have been something unusual that would drag her out to perform this ceremony. For a brief moment Jocelyn wondered what was going on and then heard the buzzer to her flat ring. Her senses immediately focused on her anticipated encounter. She casually dismissed any question she had about the motives of the Secretary.

Chapter 10

Jocelyn 5010 A.D.

Looking at herself in the mirror, she could see the ageing process taking its toll of her face. Her skin was no longer smooth and unwrinkled. There were lines beginning to appear around her eyes. The lines had the outline that a bird might make with its claws. Pretty soon the make up would no longer cover her shrinking skin. She understood she would no longer be attractive as a vibrant upcoming young woman.

That was an amusing thought because she had already risen to the top echelon of the political hierarchy so what did she have to fear.

Life would be simple if it were merely a matter of a cosmetic face lift. Unfortunately it is more complicated because there were other things going on in her body over which she had no control and for which their best medical technicians said there is no solution.

Standing in front of the full length mirror in her private quarters, she looked at herself in apprehension of what was to come. She had always been very disciplined and alone. From the time she was a little girl she knew that she was alone and would always be alone no matter how many people surrounded her or courted her company and assistance.

Women are disadvantaged when compared to men. No matter how much aerobic exercise you do, no matter what healthy diet of fruits and vegetables are eaten the aging process marches on with its own stoic confrontation. When the ovaries stop producing estrogen the body begins to feel the effect of gravity and sag into itself. First you notice your hair begin to thin, followed by the onset of bushy eyebrows and a few wild hairs sticking out of the jaw of your face. If a man's eyebrows become bushy he is considered handsome. The presence or absence of skull and body hair is not a matter noteworthy of comment. Even now the old prejudices persist.

Her breasts were beginning to sag and no longer had the elastic quality of her youth. She could see her stomach beginning to protrude out from her abdominal wall. No matter how many sit ups she did, she was unable to arrest this latest development. The solution was better uniform tailoring and more restrictive foundation garments.

She wondered what Leslie really thought. Did she remain with her because of the power and influence she wielded or was there some genuine affection on her part? The questions trouble her as she reached her 46th year.

Genetic engineering changed the social order. The nature of sexual orientation changed because male or female units could be manufactured to meet the changing needs of society. There was no longer a division of labor that was a function of sexual orientation. The division of labor was based upon functional necessity.

Of course in making gene splices the technicians always attempted to produce the brightest possible unit; however as with all things, intelligence and physical appearance took the way of the bell curve and there was great variety in the breeding outcome. The same was true for sexual preferences.

Technical advances in gene splicing rooted out the differentiation of little boys and girls, and replaced it with a more uniform measure of conduct. It was OK for boys to like boys and girls to like girls. Likewise it was OK to engage in hetro sexual enterprise because breeding and reproduction was no longer a function of the relationship between a man and a woman.

When that factor was removed, the predicate was set for a different kind of relationship to emerge because the social order was not threatened with the loss of the ensuing generation. So it was that Jocelyn had a relationship with Leslie. She chose Leslie not for her intellect but for her constant effort to please and render affection. In another age Leslie might have made a good Geisha.

The difference between her and a Geisha was that a Geisha learned her skills at the hand of a master. Leslie's physical beauty was not lost to anyone whom she came into contact with. Her golden yellow hair and pale blue eyes made a striking appearance. It was as if she could look through you and see your soul. Leslie intuitively understood her role in life. She did not have to be told what to do. She simply seemed to know what was appropriate, what was sought after and took great comfort in giving.

Many powerful people long to find themselves in an environment where they do not have to pretend they are in charge. They seek anonymity and peaceful travel. The enjoyment that comes from a beautiful person taking charge of their life, albeit in the confinement of a home or hotel room is sufficient to invigorate them to move on in their professional career. Leslie was that person. She was not an intellect. She did not care who Plato was or if President Lincoln was assassinated. Her world did not rest in the hard annals of political life. If anything it was a world punctuated with gaiety and laughter with the lady hiding behind the ivory fan. She had no political motives. Even if the nature of the state were explained to her in elementary terms, she would turn away and display no interest. She had been bred to give pleasure and extol happiness. Nothing else was of any consequence to her.

Thinking back over time, Jocelyn concluded she never took a man as a lover because she found something in the male character that sought dominance. She had never been submissive and she rebelled at the thought of a sexually dominate partner.

Jocelyn found herself beginning to question the nature of her existence. Her questions disturbed her sleep as she began to experience a gnawing anxiety that something was wrong.

Chapter 11

The Debate Revised

A bitter debate was taking place at the Central Bionics Laboratory. It revolved around the long standing feud between the medical ethicists and the Secretariat.

The medical ethicists were led by Scientist Ember Marconi. The blue veins and bursting blood vessels in her face betrayed her age. She was, after all, the grand dame of the science community in service to the State. Lately there had been rumors about her loyalty because she had raised troubling questions about human embryonic stem cell research that appeared to contradict and undermine her lifetime commitment to research in the interest of the State.

The meeting was closed to all, save Warden and Ember. No notes were to be taken, and no recordings made. Warden waited for a prearranged signal to advise her that Ember was present and then made her way into the small conference room. There were no windows in the room. The walls, door and air duct were seamless. Security was at a feverish pitch. The two women starred at each other waiting for an opening of opportunity. The silence in the room was deafening. Finally Ember took it upon herself to set the agenda.

In a quiet and controlled voice that shook with emotion she said, "Superintendent, I know you have heard some of the rumors that are circulating about me. I want to clear the air because I see us in a moral dilemma that is going to escalate out of control."

Warden took the full measure of the woman. She stared back at an old woman who had done little to preserve or enhance her physical appearance. It was as if physical appearance was of no concern to her. This was not the kind of person that Warden was used to dealing with. Most of the people who surrounded her were vain, self-centered and lacked any manner of altruistic spirit. This woman was a source of confusion. What did she really want? She presumed the best way was to keep her talking. As she peered into her face she could see her lips moving in a slow and deliberate manner as she carefully chose her words.

"I've been doing a lot of thinking about the direction of our human embryonic stem cell research. I think we have taken a wrong direction with our research and have ignored the ethical issue involved in our research."

This comment caught Warden by surprise. Suddenly there was a different level of consciousness in the room. Warden felt a tension spasm in her neck and back and waited for the next comment.

"I know we have been in a state of war with the eastern block these many years, and that we need body parts to repair injured soldiers to return them to active duty. At least this has been the theme of our research up to this point. But now this theme is no longer relevant. The advent of the Remington Blast Rifle precludes body repairs. The other side has the same technology. It's as if at an individual level every soldier has a weapon of mass destruction. Nonetheless we continue to manufacture body parts and keep them in cold storage for a repair event that is never going to take place. I am deeply troubled by the efficacy of this process because in producing these body parts we are engaging in the destruction of innocent human life. We are treating vulnerable human beings as products of the harvest."

Warden sat for ten minutes without responding. A myriad of ideas went through her head. This woman was obviously very dangerous. She had raised an issue that had long since disappeared from the litany of ethical considerations. The repercussions of the Great War brought about the necessity to harvest human stem cells in order to field the army and defend the American way of life. Religious belief and ethical claims gave way to national necessity for survival. Now this old woman wanted to open up Pandora's Box and recreate the debilitating schism of the late 20th Century. Such thoughts were not only polarizing, but were seditious and threatened to undermine the security of the State. There was no telling who she has contaminated with these ideas or what the repercussion of such ideas would be. She must be silenced, but how? Certainly not in a public debate. She could undermine the whole system of checks and balances.

When she failed to respond, Ember took it as a cue to say more.

"Harvesting human embryos is the destruction of human life. Life begins at the moment of conception, and if we treat these embryos as mere cells to be made into appendages, then we have lost all of our reverence for life and the war has no meaning. If we do not defend the defenseless what is this battle about with the eastern block?"

This was more than Warden could stomach. She did not comment on Ember's remarks.

"Who else have you discussed this with?"

"No one."

"Let's just keep this between us for the time being. I need to carefully consider what you have advised and examine possible alternatives."

"Thank you Madam Secretary."

Ember walked out of the room believing she had made a convert and that the ship of state was about to be righted.

Warden wondered if there was some middle ground that could explain away the harvesting of human body parts in a less morally repugnant way, but then thought, "It's just so many words."

Chapter 12

The Committee

The core of government was conducted at the Citadel. From the air it was not an imposing structure. It appeared as a series of tilt up concrete buildings such as would be found in an industrial park.

Grassy knolls were visible with people casually strolling the walkways that passed through the knolls. Scattered in between were a few coffee houses and benches.

A few people could be seen drinking their coffee Americano in the early morning hours before the day's business began. They seemed to emerge from nowhere and just as quickly retreat into obscurity. There were the occasional lovers who could be seen holding hands while seated on the grass, as if they had not a care in the world.

Nothing about the Citadel denoted its purpose. It was unlike the Capitol Mall of 21st Century Washington in every respect. Whereas people might gather on the Capitol Mall to protest or seek to advance a political or perceived moral cause, no such activity occurred on the grounds of the Citadel. The very existence of the Citadel was opaque to the general public. Only those with the need to know were informed of its true nature, and then only to the extent necessary for the given operation.

There was nothing about the Citadel that denoted its true purpose. Its roots extended 7,000 feet below ground into the neck of the mountain where it sat. Its many arms and hallways extended out into the countryside like an octopus. There were many people who were unaware of the existence of each other and who did not cross communicate with each other. All projects were blindfolded save for the Committee within the committee. Knowledge was closely guarded and unless there was a demonstrable need to know, knowledge was not shared.

In point of fact the Citadel was guarded from the ground and air. A complex anti-missile shield protected it from the air. Multiple batteries of artillery blast rifles weighing 200 tons were constantly on the alert for any incoming missile. Their range of fire extended for 50 miles into the atmosphere. They were powered by a nuclear electrical core some 10,000 feet below the surface of the earth. An elaborate system of tunnels reaching to the cooling waters of the ocean guaranteed continual power for the artillery blast rifles. From the air the Citadel was impregnable.

At ground level there were three Legionnaire bases that surrounded the Citadel in the shape of an isosceles triangle. Military doctrine taught that static positions were indefensible to a mobile enemy. The lesson was well known to the Legion. On any given day the Legion could field 50,000 combat ready Legionnaires from each of three points that surrounded the Citadel. These were trigger pullers, not soft support troops. They drilled everyday for conflict and relished personal combat. The officers chosen to lead each platoon were carefully selected based on their genetic profile and progress in the mastery of military doctrine. Each knew he was expendable and loyalty was to the mother Secretariat. The pledge to the Secretariat was not simply a linguistic anachronism. It was indelibly etched into the psyche.

The Legion was prepared for classical war and asymmetrical revolution. The nature of the conflict was of no consequence.

A 21ˢt Century American would have reeled from the closed nature of government in the 51ˢᵗ Century. Such governance was repugnant to everything that so many of our ancestors believed in. To the 51ˢᵗ Century American, life was normal and good. Anyone who challenged the established social order must be a subversive or suffer from an incurable social affliction.

In old Washington it was hard to keep a secret. There was always someone ready to gore your ox. The press acted as the third estate should and held the politicians' feet to the fire. Little escaped public scrutiny. Certainly nothing was sacred. Politicians who said, "I did not have sex with that woman," had to face the tests of her clothing that detected the presence of seminal fluid. Whether this was right or wrong was not the issue.

The press maintained there was a social contract that read if the politicians misbehaved they could be thrown out as bums. At the very least they would be exposed to withering public inspection of their affairs. In the sense that 21st Century Washington was filled with conflicting view points and social intrigue the affairs of state of the 51st Century were no different. The cast of rogues had changed but the fuel that ran the carriage of state remained much the same.

Garrett Winslow found himself in the unenviable position of being an observer in the affairs of state. It was not a position he coveted. Affairs of state are always filled with intrigue. In the quest for power there is always one person or group that seeks dominance or currie's favor to the disadvantage of another. If there is a unified national purpose, the damage is minimal. If there is a basic difference in the tone and objective of the policy, whether it be foreign or domestic the danger is great.

As a country we remained a unified people because dissent had been stifled since the middle of the 21st Century. Chaos and destruction following the great attack brought about personal uncertainty and political instability in the middle of the 21st Century. As a consequence certain politicians garnered power and the Secretariat came into being.

Violence in the streets was replaced with domestic tranquility. All that the populace had to be concerned with were foreign enemies. Advances in genetic engineering virtually assured a lengthened life period. Body parts wore out, but were replaced from embryonic stem cells that were specially cultivated for repair purposes.

There was no public outcry over the use of stem cells from the medical ethicists. It was taken as a given that the preservation of existing sentient life took precedence over a mindless ova that had been fertilized.

Eventually the world divided into two recognizable camps. Humanity seemed to need an enemy, although it is not clear there was any longer a real difference between America and the eastern block. As time went on America developed a new ideology and philosophy. Somewhere along the way it stopped recognizing the uniqueness of the individual and the Republican form of government. These concepts were lost in the necessity to keep things moving.

The Secretariat became the sole center of power, and the trains ran on time. Population was limited by the needs of the State to the number of units necessary for any given situation. There was no dissent. It was not necessary to burn any books because the only volumes read dealt with technical matters as opposed to humanitarian issues. Besides that, books were no longer printed, and were only available in electronic format. Easily revised to suit the occasion and needs of the Secretariat.

Of course the Inner Circle of the Secretariat always worried that an abreaction or oddity would occur and some fool would read the old books and challenge the existing social order. That did not happen for 3,000 years. The demon was purely mythological, and no one save the Inner Circle had explored the world of ideas for all these years.

Those in the outer circle knew where their bread was buttered and that to engage in seditious conduct would bring severe personal sanctions. Life went on as a wheel. It was not necessary to dispense tranquilizers to the population as a whole because life with exception of the Legion was tranquil. Sometimes violent events took place between individuals but the authority of the state was never challenged.

America had finally become a society of technocrats who understood welfare and happiness depended on continued acceptable performance. Good and evil were eliminated from the lexicon because there was no necessity for the concepts to co-exist with each other.

In another life, Garrett Winslow would have been called a "nerd." He was of medium build with brown hair and brown eyes. He would not stand out in a crowd, nor was he distinguishable in any manner. Garrett was a software engineer who programmed the computers of the Secretariat and kept things going on an even keel.

He was not particularly fond of people and preferred to work in the deep recesses of the building, carefully cultivating his machines. It was not that he disliked people, he simply lacked the social skills to communicate with the people around him. Programming was entirely different and predictable.

Garrett never fancied himself a revolutionary, and in point of fact had never been with a man or woman. He was after all a 28 year old virgin, and would probably die as a 150 year old virgin. He could not imagine himself in an intimate relationship with another person. The thought of physical contact was alien to him, not because he disliked people, but because he had no sense of intimacy. He was alone and detached in the same manner of disengagement as one of his beloved computers.

He believed he lacked a soul and that none would be forthcoming to him. It was a lonely life, but he did not know he was alone. He was alive, but could not articulate the consciousness of his existence. He could sense other people and objects in his immediate and distant environment but felt nothing. He was part of the landscape but detached from the reality of life.

Today he sensed that something strange was taking place. He was asked to make a repair call to the Secretariat's office. There was an idea floating around. He saw it in the memory bank of her computer. Perhaps he should not have been there. The indication was the Secretariat intended to engage the eastern block in order to start a new page in bilateral relations. What did this engagement mean? From poking around the computers for the last 6 years he had a fund of knowledge as to what was really going on in the world. By himself he lacked the courage to reveal his knowledge or act upon it. It struck him as naive that the Secretariat would seek to engage in a new page with the eastern block when it was clear that the eastern block had no intention of reaching an accommodation with the west and in fact was only bent on the destruction of the west. For the first time in his life he began to question the assumptions of the Secretariat and State. He found himself in a horrible state of mental conflict and was unable to sleep. His placid world was turning into a nightmare.

Chapter 13

High Anxiety

Jocelyn found herself tossing from side to side. Sleep would not come. She thought about the mental place she usually journeyed to when every thing was closing in on her. That usually allowed her to withdraw and pass into a deep state of unconsciousness.

She briefly remembered the pleasure she had from putting her face in Leslie's lap as she gently messaged her back and she passed into a protected sleep. Tonight sleep would not come. There was no refuge in her safe memory.

The satin sheets felt hot and moist. Perching up on her side she looked at the wall mount. It was pitch black in the room save for the tiny diode illuminated by the instruments of the wall mount. The clock showed it was 3:35 a.m. The temperature was a perfect 68 degrees. Still she felt hot with a head that was heavy from the day's problems.

The problems were becoming insurmountable and they seemed to multiply at a geometric pace. It was possible to delegate most matters but some she had to take personal responsibility for and of course could confide in no one lest she be betrayed. The affairs of state sat heavy on her head.

Advisors were not to be trusted because each had her own agenda. In a more democratic society there would be checks and balances circumventing the perils of absolute rule. In her society there were simply the technocrats who interpreted the rules to self-advantage. In the overall scheme of things, it did not matter because electricity was delivered on time, clean water was available to all, and food was plentiful.

No one indulged in the fanciful concept of the soul and instead relegated it to a more primitive time in our historical development. People were developed as units and within the framework of a peaceful society units coexisted within the rules until they wore out and were replaced.

The notion of romantic love and lifetime commitment long ago ceased to have any relevance to everyday life.

When thinking about romantic love Jocelyn found herself amused. She remembered that time 34 years before when she was eleven years old. She was in the dormitory shower and her hand instinctively went to her privates to wash herself. Without knowing why she began to explore her inner self and discovered there was more to her pee hole than a functional urine drain.

As she moved her hand around she experienced pleasurable sensations in her privates that impacted her for the remainder of her life. She realized she could do this for herself without the aid of anyone else. She was in fact empowered with a startling new discovery. She began to massage her public area in a rhythmic motion and at the same time contracted her pelvic muscles. Organism in the past had always worked to send her into a restful mental oblivion. Tonight it failed. She could not bring herself to come.

Her mind was gripped with the icy feeling of fear. Fear is the thief of confidence. Fear destroys good order. Fear creates uncertainty. It is linear and exponential and detracts from the constant motion of the wheel. She suddenly realized what she had to do but it would be with great difficulty.

Chapter 14

The Inner Circle

Sitting at the conference table Gunter Ras found it difficult to appreciate the muddled voices of concern that barely echoed through the chamber.

The faces looked old and weary, and seemed to match the muffled sounds from the talking heads. There did not appear to be any coherent idea being voiced from the participants. It was as if there was a state of mental panic and no reasonable solutions were tendered for consideration. Was this the august council where all authority was reposed or was it simply a body of elderly people who remained in power beyond their productive years?

The thought crossed his mind as he gazed out across the Group of 14 at the round table.

The only person who seemed distinguishable from the group was the Secretary. Out of the corner of his eye he caught her taking the full measure of the assembly and wondered about her thoughts.

More than that it occurred to him that perhaps she wanted the Chamber to remain a politic of old people so that her iron grip on life was not challenged. That too occurred to him, but if this were the case, why was he allowed to be a member of this distinguished group? It puzzled him a great deal.

The level of senseless buzz in the room raised his hearing to a level of perception he had not previously experienced. He could feel his anxiety heighten and instinctively recognized that decisive action was mandated. He kept asking himself, should I reveal who I am, is the price too high?

As if without an afterthought, he found himself standing looking down at the assemblage. The room began to still, and all eyes started to focus in his direction. He knew it was important to carefully choose his words because in the angst of the day, what he said could be used against him.

Standing there, the past week flashed before him with all the doubts and fears that men carry in their innermost thoughts, but he knew that the time had come if he was to claim a leadership position.

"My friends, I have given a great deal of thought to our problem. It occurs to me that the nature of the political system makes no difference to the ordinary person because in the smallest sense that person's universe is the principal of self-interest that completely dictates outcome.

"As long as a unit has a bowl of rice, clothing and personal safety the chances of that unit becoming a revolutionary are slim to none. In other words the nature of the political system is no consequence assuming the system guarantees certain fundamental rights. Our society is really very simple. We have done away with the nuclear family, hence marriage and the raising of children is no longer a viable anxiety. Within limits we genetically enhance units to perform specific jobs which are necessary to the preservation of good order and the society. Our society is no longer dependent on the outmoded notion of the nuclear family because selective laboratory breeding and bringing up children in "Kinder Hauses" has proven to be a more productive environment that produces a non-neurotic and rational unit. Likewise, in the last thousand years we have been able to escape from the primitive notion that units have a soul imparted through God. We know that we are simply the highest order in the biological food chain."

He saw a lot of heads nodding in assent, but the icy stare of the Secretary was disconcerting.

Finally he got to the point. "So what if a few nerds are poking through the master historical computer at the Library of Congress? What can they possibly discover that would be harmful to our society? I go back to the premise that as long as a man has his bowl of rice he will not become a revolutionary. We have nothing to fear from a bunch of old ideas."

With that he sat down to the applause in the room.

Chapter 15

Gaul and Jocelyn

Gaul and Jocelyn walked out of the meeting of the Inner Circle. Throughout the meeting he had taken her measure as a woman. He was intrigued with the thought that here was an age equivalent woman who was obviously very smart. He did not feel threatened by her intelligence or position.

Instead it egged him on to know more about her. He had grown weary of the cute little spinners whose life experience was a thimble, and who were only attracted to him because of his station in life.

In a sense he had become weary from the process of living. He wanted someone to see him for who he really was, not for the power that he held. Jocelyn by all standards was an attractive woman. True her girly days were long gone, but who wants to play to a silly choir.

He wondered what the basis of attraction was between a mature man and woman. It had surely eluded all of the writers he had experienced in the Library. As they walked out of the meeting, he brushed up against her.

"Sorry, I didn't mean to bump into you."

She slowly turned and looked at him. In this moment of time he was stripped naked of his mask. It was as if she looked through him and saw the inner core. She gave him a little smile.

"It's OK, nothing happened."

From deep inside of her she felt a fire welling up. She had never felt this kind of emotion before. She wondered why now; after all she had nothing in common with Gaul.

"Hey, I was just thinking, are you hungry or maybe you want a drink?"

Gaul found himself acting like a 16 year old without social skills or experiences. He did not want to let her go and lose the moment.

"Yeah, I could eat something."

They exited the meeting place and took a flyer to Mario's Steak House. Mario's was more then a mere steak house. Its balcony stood high above the city skyline. It was a place of pleasure and a place to be seen.

Without thinking he reached out to grab her hand and lead her into the restaurant. It seemed like the natural thing to do. He wanted to touch her and see what she felt like. Surprisingly she offered no resistance. He could smell the gentle wisps of perfume on her body. He had heard rumors that she was involved in a lesbian relationship, but that mattered little to him. He viewed such relationships as childish exploration of one's sexuality that bore no real resemblance to personality.

Looking at him caused her to wonder what this man wanted from her. She thought of herself in a stable relationship, at least for the time being, and really had no place for this man. Still, she found him attractive and was flattered by his attention.

For his part he wanted to explore the mind behind her face. They talked about everything except themselves. His was a mission of exploration. He kept returning to the thought that puzzled him so much. Why was he attracted to this woman? They did not seem to run out of things to talk about. Then there were the looks. When he turned away he could feel her staring into his presence. He too was guilty of the same conduct. Something strange was happening to them.

Abruptly he got up.

"I have to leave. It's been very nice chatting with you. Perhaps we will do it again."

Jocelyn was immediately disappointed. She thought, "Am I so dull that he dispensed with me in an hour?"

Insecurity gnawed at her core. Perhaps it was safer to just drop the matter and rely on Leslie for warmth and affection. Then again she was self-sufficient. She never really relied on anyone for warmth and affection. They just used each other in a symbiotic sort of a relationship. She felt like the Gods were pissing on her, if there were Gods.

They both walked away, each in their own world. Gaul thought to himself that with the upcoming crisis he could not afford to divert his attention to a woman. Such conduct was illogical and made no sense to him. Conversely he recognized that this woman brought out something in him that he did not know previously existed. It was a dichotomy that offered no direction. If he were to stand for something, this woman could be an impediment. Men with lovers do not make good revolutionaries because they fear taking the kind of risks that are necessary to sustain the revolution. On the other hand maybe there was something to be said for defending motherhood, apple pie and the flag. It all gave him a very uneasy feeling.

Chapter 16

Gunter Ras

In a perfect world, Gunter Ras would have made a good "buck sergeant." By no stretch of the imagination would he ever rise to the rank of a "Gunney," because he lacked the compassion and insight to lead. All things being said there was a place for men of his kind.

He was slightly above normal in intelligence and very crafty. What he lacked in intellect he more than made up for in suspicion and stealth. More importantly he did not question orders.

He had an abiding dislike of anyone who challenged the established order. He prized himself on his good looks and obedience to command. He was dismissive of anyone who scratched below the surface to see what lurks below.

He was the perfect wooden soldier, the ideal candidate for promotion to the Committee of the Inner Circle. He could be trusted to carry out any order without questioning its correctness or moral grounding. That is not to say that he was duplicitous. He was simply who he was without fanfare and adulation. A cog in the mighty wheel of government.

He was best described as a true believer, an adherent to the cause without room for dissuasion by any facts contrary to what had been ingrained in his psyche.

Gunter believed that physical fitness was more important than social studies devoted to the dead facts of history.

What was important was a physically healthy individual with a firm character committed to the preservation of the Secretariat. If he had been familiar with the concept of an "intellectual individual" he would have discarded the person as unfit for the good of the community. He believed what he was told and looked to emerge from his training to the top level of the Secretariat. He viewed his existence as a precious gift to the human genome.

His kind would make the margin of difference in the rough world of the 51st Century. There is always room for Gunter's type of person because such people never challenge the existing social order. They become a part of the wallpaper and mimic the social rules. They are dangerous because they rise to power on an opaque wave that does not confront issues. For this kind of person there are no issues.

In the crudest sense they simply suck up to the strong and powerful and flatter them with a spirit of adulation. Most rational people enjoy a favorable social comment. Powerful people crave flattery because it justifies their inflated sense of proportion. At an elemental level Gunter understood this principal and was determined to act upon it to his advantage.

He was not an inherently evil man. He was simply a man with wants and needs who early on took stock of his resources and elected to act upon them. He used to say to himself, "That woman is standing in my way to success, I need to figure out how to get rid of her." That is the way he approached life. When Gunter finished his education at the Health Science Institute he was required to write a paper as a condition to matriculation.

His primary interest was in genetics and gene splicing for the purpose of creating a more physically stable species. He requested permission to spend six months at the laboratory of the Health Science Institute in order to observe the ongoing research and techniques. His request was received at the Secretariat and quickly approved. Everyday he would rise at 5 a.m. and go to the laboratory.

Chapter 17

The Revolution

Whoever said that revolutions start because of oppression was wrong. Suppressed masses rarely exert themselves on their own. They are essentially lethargic and uninformed as to a better way of life. Revolutions start with an idea that infects the existing social order. Change is brought about through the disorderly process of exchanging new ideas.

If there is no infection (inspiration from the outside or above) the daily lethargy goes on. Life is a wheel without beginning or end. Infect the mind of a man and a curious creature is released from the bottle. This innate curiosity distinguishes mankind from the rest of the creatures in the evolutionary chain. Curiosity involves the ability to look from side to side, backward and forward and then to compare. In the course of comparison, new ideas emerge.

The 51st Century was no different than any other period in the history of the human race. Throughout recorded history there were dark times, and periods of enlightenment.

Technology does not equate with enlightenment. 51st Century technology was a thin veneer of achievement that advanced the ability to produce food, harvest resources and engage in horrific brutality and war. It did not advance the human condition.

Following the Great War, the conflict persisted as a low grade engagement for 3,000 years. Rules of war and engagement emerged. The most important rule was that cities could not be bombed by an airship. The toll of death and destruction was too great to allow this to happen. Open cities were indefensible. Force fields to repel invading missiles never developed as a technology. Anti-Missile defense was never able to counter the thousands of incoming strikes.

In a sense the parties were forced to re-adopt the rules of the Cold War; that any nuclear engagement would result in the destruction of all parties, and therefore it was in their mutual interest not to bomb from the air. Engagements were limited to small ground skirmishes where one side viewed its interest compromised by conduct of the other side. Heavy casualties were eliminated.

A balance of terror began to emerge. There were the usual cases of espionage and technology theft but by and large the balance held. Full scale war as an alternative to political policy was an untenable concept. Institutions within New America became bureaucratic centers of power. If you were lucky enough to have gotten the good gene splice at the time of conception, life was good. Progress was defined in terms of scientific advancement. Keeping the country safe from external forces was not merely a motto but was in fact the ethic of the population.

Along the way, the humanities ceased to exist. All concentration was on survival of the American way of life. No one ever bothered to articulate what that way of life was or what the promise of America was. The schools stopped teaching children to play musical instruments.

Beethoven, Brahmas and Schumann were relegated to the dusty basement of the storage facility, and ultimately their sound was not heard. Survival and the war were the driving factors of the nation. Anything that could contribute to the repopulation of America was considered good. Microbiology, genetics and computer modeling were encouraged and supported by the government.

Theater, the arts and literature were at first abandoned because each in its own way lacked any relevance to preservation of the nation state, and because people were so frightened by the fear of complete national collapse, that all effort was directed to the war effort.

Slowly the lights went out of the humanities departments on the university campuses. Eventually there was complete darkness.

History began and ended with the Great War. The Magna Carter and the writings of Thomas Paine passed into oblivion. It was as if they had never existed; worst of all no one complained of their absence.

America changed because of the attack. Washington was gone. The system of bicameral government that had lasted for more then 250 years faded into obscurity. Most of the population in the states on the east and west coast of North America died from the initial attack. In California there were 31,000,000 dead. Nothing survived.

The President convened a gathering of the remaining life science experts in America. The conference was held on the campus of John's Hopkins Hospital in Baltimore. It was fitting that such a conference be held there because this was an institution dedicated to the preservation of life.

Before the conference took place he met with his remaining advisors. The meeting began with the President saying God bless the United States of America. His voice trembled as he said the words, but he knew he had to stand tall and lead a broken people. The eyes of the country were on him. Aboard Air Force One, a hushed meeting was taking place between the President and Secretary of State.

"Madam Secretary, I cannot conceive of a more perilous time in America. We have to act to preserve what is left of the country. The Congress is gone, as are half the states and large population centers. We cannot continue to do business as if nothing were changed. You were always concerned with health care and the welfare of the people. I have a bigger issue for you now. How do we perpetuate American life and the American way of life? I want you to direct all of your energies to this issue and come up with a detailed plan within the next 72 hours. This country must survive. Failure is not an option. Our heritage must be preserved. God bless the United States of America."

On that note he retired to his private quarters. The Secretary sat transfixed for a long time. The crushing affairs of state had fallen on her desk. She would be responsible for molding the shape of the country for the next 3,000 years. Responsibility weighed heavily on her shoulders. The responsibility did not matter, she loved power. She loved the exercise of authority. Now absolute power had been delegated to her. She wondered how she would be remembered. Would she be remembered as the woman who fought for universal health care or as a capricious villain who only acted in her own self-interest? She knew that she was neither. Sometimes historical events simply overtook the individual.

Chapter 18

Confusion

Gaul returned to the Library many times. He was steadily rising in the rank of the Legion and no longer had to manufacture excuses for his absence.

He explained his trips to the desert as the need for abstinence from the worldly pleasures of food and sex. In reality he was pursuing what would eventually become a spiritual goal, but which was not readily apparent to him from the outset.

Asceticism as a concept was foreign to Gaul. He found little pleasure in the daily ingestion of food and experiences of the skin. Perhaps it was the complete availability of warm sensation without commitment that troubled him. In the inner recesses of his mind, he sensed that a vital link was missing because his life was without purpose other than to endure. Merely to endure was not enough for him.

In the memory of his ear he could hear the thunderous sounds of the Beethoven 9th and knew he must discover this lost world. The Seniors on the Council watched him from the distance. They thought his conduct of slipping off into the desert was odd but not heretical. Perhaps his gene pool reflected a need for self-reflection that would manifest itself in higher achievement. They resolved to leave him alone in the belief that no harm was being done. His behavior was merely an oddity explainable by lack of complete genetic programming.

When he returned to the Library, Gaul initially took to fasting as a way of coming in contact with his inner self. In depriving himself of food he sought to look within himself and find some hidden meaning that had not been revealed to him. Three days of fasting without water in the desert caused him to hallucinate that he was having a conversation with God.

On waking he realized he had to eat and drink and that the road to discovery did not lie in the inner recesses of his mind, but rather in the external sources of information in the Library.

It suddenly occurred to him that seeking pleasure for its own sake was not pleasurable but doing so in a spiritual way presented a different reward. He asked himself the question, "Do I thank God for the good food that I eat, or do I thank the Secretariat? Who do I thank for the pleasures of sex?"

Gaul was shaken by his own reference to God. It was confusing to him that in the emblem of the Secretariat it said "In God We Trust." Why would anyone trust in God when all good was derived from the Secretariat? The questions and linguistics made no sense to him. Worst of all he had no one to talk to in order to challenge his thoughts. He could not write them at his computer terminal because they would be seen and he would be exposed.

He began to live in his own inferno. He understood that to abstain from good food, sex and pleasurable activities did not enhance his inner self or assuage the growing fear inside of him. He was beginning to develop a thirst for historical knowledge. He wanted to know who came before him, what his ideas were and where his life was going. This was all new for Gaul, unproven ground that challenged his every life assumption.

Gaul matured as a man. In a sense he was untouchable. He was feared by many and hated by all. He had no friends, only continuing short alliances based on common interests. Sex had become a matter of mere physical affirmation.

Masturbation would have been preferable, but he lacked the ability to fantasize an intimate relationship with a woman.

He had begun to read voraciously. The Library became his source of pleasure. At first it was hit or miss. He read several works of fiction, but found them to be a dead end. Sweet stories of romance in an age long dead. An age of chivalry and paresoles with wooden characters that bore no resemblance to real life. His search remained constant.

He recognized that somewhere in this vast arcade there was a book or series of books that objectively revealed the history of mankind. The question was where to look because the Library was so vast. As with everything else there is always a first revelation. Quite by accident he came across a series of books entitled "The Story of Civilization" by Will Durant. He had discovered the Rosetta Stone.

He read and read and read. He did not stop to eat or drink, but simply absorbed for four days without stop. In the end he was exhausted and fell into a deep slumber. Upon awakening his head felt like a watermelon. He thought his body had been run over by a tractor.

It did not matter. Knowledge is power and now he knew where he was going. His quest had direction, meaning and purpose, and although he did not have a clear objective he believed it would be revealed in time.

Chapter 19

Gaul and Jocelyn

The life of a general is a lonely experience. Command is always a difficult thing. You can never really make friends with people that you may sacrifice at some later point in time. To befriend them is to betray yourself.

Command requires detachment, some self-reflection and no self-doubt. If doubt creeps in it is like a cancer that eats away at confidence and eventually destroys the ability to lead. That is not to say that a commander must be cold blooded. There must always be a certain amount of care for one's subordinates, and certainly for the belief in their victory.

However the effect of command is to place the commander in mental isolation. It is not that he cannot trust anyone, it is that he must not become involved at a life status value with those he will ask to die. It is better to simply know them as numbers and ranks. To personalize them with names and remember their faces is to undermine the effectiveness to lead. Command is a lonely place. It is solitary.

You cannot ask anyone what they think of your decisions because that empowers them to undermine the decisions. It is a solitary world where only the strongest or most insane survive. Gaul felt the pain of isolation. He had no one to share his thoughts with. He feared that if he were to disclose anything the revolt would be endangered and that this Dark Age would last forever. He balanced his personal needs against his belief in the revolution. There was no choice but to maintain his personal isolation.

In his mind he tried to find a reasonable alternative to his crises of confidence in the Secretariat. There was no one to go to. He could not complain to the Secretariat about the abuse of power because it was the body politic that was engaging in the abuse. He could not take his case to the people because the people had no concept of political rights.

The Secretariat used its political power to suppress all dissent, and he could see that it would never peacefully cede power to the people even if the people were prepared to accept power. There could not be a struggle for a just and democratic society because the people had no concept of what a democratic society was. They merely accepted what was in place.

Justice and/or equality were foreign concepts that were nonexistent in the lexicon. It was a very dark age. Gaul struggled with the problem. In reading the old writings he came across the notion that all human beings have certain natural inalienable rights and that the design of civil government cannot be to deprive the people of these rights, or take away their liberty or freedom. Government existed to protect the people in the enjoyment of liberty.

Gaul could see that democracy practiced on a large scale was messy and that there would always be many competing interest groups once the genie was out of the bottle. He read more and came to the conclusion that the old assumptions were correct. If the government becomes capricious and tyrannical, the government forfeits its right to legitimacy and the people have the right to revolt against such tyrants. Gaul had now become a committed revolutionary.

Now he was the intellect, commander and revolutionary. He felt himself going insane from his sense of social responsibility to champion the cause of free men. He kept saying to himself, "How do I light the world? How do I turn on the torch? How can I recreate the values of a long dead past in this dark world of ours?"

Sometimes even brilliant men play with fire. There is a need to see how close to the edge of the abyss you can come before falling off.

Gaul was no different. He met Jocelyn Jones at a meeting of the Inner Circle. He was attracted to her not because of her looks, but because he sensed something about her that intrigued him. The rules of attraction between human beings are strange. There was something about her that he found vibrant. Perhaps it was because she did not seek to attract him. He had heard rumors that she was only into women but being a man this thought was of little consequence. Men think with their dicks! The old saying is that the little head rules the big head. If biology was a guide Gaul was no different.

He wanted to explore this woman and see who she really was. How could he do that without drawing attention to himself and to her? He wondered if she really had a brain or whether she was just one more piece of fluff that had been promoted to the Inner Circle because of the necessity to have another woman on the council. Testosterone does strange things to the brain. Some say it impedes neural activity, while others maintain it stimulates the thought process. In Gaul's case it was neither. He did not fancy himself stuck in the sack with a 46 year old snoring woman. That was what he thought as he looked at her. On the other hand, he perceived the glimmer of a first-class mind, and he wondered if he could corrupt it to join the conspiracy. It was a dubious question that would portend terrible consequences for many people.

How do you communicate with such a woman? Gaul gave it a great deal of thought. It occurred to him to leave an abbreviated copy of Thomas Paine's "Rights of Man" in her apartment.

Access to her apartment was easy. As he slipped the bolt and entered, he marveled at the gentle appearance of the rooms. The rooms were painted in soft hues reflecting the gentle side of Jocelyn. This was a side that she seldom displayed in public. He quickly dropped the pamphlet on her nightstand and exited the building. She never saw the pamphlet before her arrest.

Chapter 20

The Inner Circle

Secretary Warden called the meeting of the Inner Circle to order. This was to be a full meeting of the Inner Circle with all major and minor dignitaries present.

Gunter Ras sat to her right. An obvious measure of the power he now exercised. The table of the Chamber was round so as to symbolize the equal sharing of power. In practice there was no equal sharing.

There were 13 chairs around the table symbolic of the 13 states in the Articles of Confederation, plus one additional chair for Secretary Warden. Given the narrow expanse of territory that was now the New North America the symbolism was apparent to all.

The Secretariat had become an autocracy of sorts. All real political power was concentrated in the hands of Secretary Warden, save what she would delegate and dole out to the remaining members of the Inner Circle. She was not a despot, tyrant or dictator. The Inner Circle was not a South American Junta where the members stood around in black sunglasses fondling their UZI machine pistols.

Secretary Warden recognized that she did not have the personal charisma and skills to run every facet of government, nor was it her proclivity to do so. She fancied herself a manager of a political power structure and that she had been entrusted to guard this government against all enemies, domestic and foreign.

She viewed herself as a citizen of the United States, a country with superior values, and technology. Her ascendancy to power was an inherent birthright owing to superior gene selection and achievement. Her national purpose was to uphold the lives of all Americans save and except those of the Legion. The Legion was a renewable resource and an expendable commodity.

She was the product of 3,000 years of proven genetic engineering. It never occurred to her that people should have the right to choose their own governor, or that governors should be cashiered for misconduct. Most importantly it did not occur to her that the people had a right to frame the government for themselves. These were alien concepts. While she was aware of the concepts at a conceptual level she totally rejected them.

In her world all that really mattered was the preservation of the nation state, albeit at the expense of the individual. She was unamenable to the constitutional concept that all men are created equal, and are endowed with certain inalienable rights. To her way of thinking a person's rights were no greater than the slice of DNA that went into his or her construction.

The mutations for genetic gene splicing were incalculable. Her's was a bio world devoid of humanistic energy. Its sole purpose was to perpetuate itself, without social objective beyond survival.

Gaul sat five chairs away from Superintendent Warden. He appeared to neither look to the right or left, but merely maintained his composure. He was the great sphinx in the meeting. Out of the corner of his eye he carefully observed Gunter Ras. Ras was paying no heed to the Superintendent. Ras' attention was focused on Jocelyn Jones. It was rumored that Jocelyn was slated to replace the Chairman when she elected Senior Status. Ras was eyeing her as if he wanted to turn her over, bend her down and fuck her on the table.

Gaul was amused by his own thought and the projection of that thought onto Ras. He thought, "My mind must be playing tricks on me." For her part Jocelyn hardly noticed that Ras existed.

Stories that circulated about her said that she preferred women as sexual partners to men. Gaul did not know if that was true or not. Jocelyn intrigued him because aside from being a fine looking woman she portended to have great power. Not a person to offend or ignore. Gaul wondered what she tasted like.

Catching himself in such a licentious thought, he quickly moved to ignore her. For her part Jocelyn was acutely aware of the attention that was being paid to her. She always enjoyed being the center of attention, but did not covet sexual activity with a man because she would never surrender her freedom of movement to any man. The thought of a man lying on top of her was repugnant. Sex is a matter of perception.

Never say never! You never know what is going to happen. Chairman Warden began by invoking God to bless the assembly. Jocelyn wondered what God had to do with this assembly. In her mind she could find no rational explanation.

Chapter 21

The Sneak

Gunter Ras above all else was a sneak. Secretary Warden was sufficiently paranoid to believe that someone in the Inner Circle was after her position. She never conceived that anyone would try and overthrow the Secretariat. After all it had existed for 3,000 years in an undisturbed manner.

There was good order to the system. The trains ran on time, and every man had his bowl of rice. The country was not ripe for revolution. Nonetheless she trusted no one. She called Gunter into her private chambers.

"I want you to conduct a search of the living quarters of every member of the Inner Council."

"What am I looking for?"

"Anything suspicious!"

Her orders were general enough to satisfy Gunter.

Entering Jocelyn's apartment was easy enough. Looking though it gave him a sense of power. It was a rush. Opening drawers and removing intimate garments heightened his sense of power. If only he could find something significant. He looked all over and observed nothing of interest. Everything appeared to be ordinary. In many ways Jocelyn lived a pedestrian existence.

As he was about to leave some papers caught his eye. Walking over to inspect them, he realized it was an old pamphlet. The English script that was used appeared foreign to his eyes. He wondered what she was doing with something that appeared to be so old.

He picked up the pamphlet and began to read. As he silently examined the words he knew that he had made a great find. Jocelyn Jones was the ultimate subversive. She was a disciple of Thomas Paine. She subscribed to the idea that government was to serve the people and that if it did not, the bums should be thrown out. This was not merely heresy, it was malicious sedition. He quickly grabbed the pamphlet and requested an immediate audience with the Chairman.

Chairman Warden listened intently to his report. She picked up the pamphlet in her hand and quickly discarded it as if were laced with a loathsome disease.

"Who else knows about this matter?"

"No one Madam Secretary."

"Keep it to yourself! I want you to pick up Jocelyn's friends and take them into custody. We have to know how far this conduct of hers has gone. Don't kill them, what we need now is information. Once we have sucked them dry, you can do as you will to dispose of them."

Gunter understood what he had to do. His first step was to arrest all of the staffers of Jocelyn and take them into remote custody.

"It must appear that they have simply taken a vacation from their jobs. Nothing must appear to be disturbed. Also, Jocelyn's lover Leslie Marcus must be taken into immediate custody and interrogated."

He relished the idea of questioning her. He would do her himself.

Chapter 22

Leslie Marcus

Hearing the heavy pounding on her door startled Leslie out of her deep sleep. She reached to the side of bed and pulled on her robe and went to the door. The pounding was incessant. She worried there was a fire in the building or that someone was hurt.

She reached the door and unlatched the lock. At about the same time as she was unlatching the door, she heard a heavy pounding as if from a large hammer and the door flung open and struck her in the face. The force of the impact broke her nose and she could feel the blood streaming out of her nostrils and trickling down the inside of her throat.

She observed six heavily armed men at her door, two of them holding a large metal battering-ram that had been used on the door, and the others holding Remington Blast Rifles. She was in a state of bewilderment. Nothing in her past life had prepared her for this experience. She could not understand what these soldiers were doing at her door.

In looking at their uniforms she saw they were from the Internal Security Police. That was all the more confusing to her because she had nothing to do with any government agency. She was simply a citizen who was not involved in any way.

"Leslie Marcus, we have a warrant for your arrest. Come with us." She could not believe what she was hearing. She felt the grip of a strong hand swing her about and handcuff her. She was led to a waiting vehicle and whooshed off to a prison compound. As they traveled on the deserted road she started to cry.

"Why are you arresting me, what am I accused of?"

"All in good time. Be quiet!"

As if to emphasize the necessity for her silence the policeman to her right smacked her in the mouth with his gloved hand. She could feel the inside of her lip as it was penetrated by her right incisor. It felt as if they had traveled for hours. The reality was that they took her to a small compound that sat in a heavily wooded grove in the forest. The compound was away from all peering eyes and listening ears.

They roughly dragged her out of the vehicle and strapped her to a chair. She could feel the terror well up in her. She kept thinking, "What do they believe I have done? Who are these men?"

Another large ground vehicle pulled up. It was deep black and the windows were opaque. She could not see who was in the vehicle. It stood there for a long time, and then the door opened. Out stepped an officer of the General Staff. She immediately recognized him as Gunter Ras.

"Gunter, Gunter, help me please! These men have taken me for no reason. Please, please help me. You know me, I am no criminal." Gunter looked at her with the calm reflection of a man engaged in an evil enterprise.

"Tell me who your co-conspirators are and I will let you go. If you fail to tell me I cannot help you."

Leslie looked at him with a dumbfounded expression. She did not know how to answer him. What was he talking about? How could he do this to her? How could he think such bad thoughts of her? Why would he allow this to happen?

"Gunter, I beg you, call Jocelyn, she will clear all of this up."

Leslie had unwittingly become a player in the game without knowing what the game was all about. Gunter nodded to one of the guards. He began to hit Leslie with a lead sap. At first his blows were confined to her arms and shoulders. With each blow the strength seemed to ebb out of her body.

"Leslie, do you want to talk? Now is the time. It is now or never!"

Leslie's body was racked with pain. She knew she could not take much more of this punishment. She also understood the finality of his words. She had seen Gunter in social situations at the Citadel and knew he was a man of little flexibility. There was no one to cry out to. No one would hear her fall in the forest.

"Gunter, I am only 25, I've not lived yet. Please let me live. Please do not kill me."

With that Gunter turned to his henchman and lifted his finger to his face. The henchman began to beat Leslie around the head with his lead sap. He kept hitting her until her voice was silent. Her face hardly resembled the beautiful Leslie. The person who had given so much pleasure to Jocelyn was no more. Her voice was silent.

Gunter Ras had learned nothing from his brave act. It was clear to all those present that he was a coward. The problem was they were all cowards, only able to murder defenseless women. Judgment day would come for the bastards!

They burned the remains of Leslie for fear that her body would be discovered revealing their crime. Gunter was careful to order the assination of each man involved in the incident. He did not want any trail coming back to himself. Leslie Marcus became a disappeared person. She might well have been living in a banana republic in the 20th Century rather than 51st Century America for all the difference it made.

Chapter 23

Gunter Ras the Artist

In his own way Gunter Ras was an accomplished artist. In a more enlightened age his water colors would be welcomed for their vibrancy and the warm feelings they conveyed. It was as if there were two Gunters. Gunter the toy soldier and Gunter the great artist. The dominant personality was the toy soldier.

In the secrecy of his apartment he painted. His subjects were abstract and distant. It was as if he was looking into another universe. Occasionally he would paint floral designs. When he did, he had great difficulty in overcoming the warmth they conveyed. He was fearful of their warmth, and preferred the cold stare into the void. Had he been encouraged to express himself he would have been a different man. As it was he hid his painting from all out of fear that his talent would be perceived as weakness.

Chapter 24

The Trial of Jocelyn Jones

Jocelyn Jones was charged with crimes of high treason. The certain penalty, death by hanging.

As she sat in her cell, she wondered, "What is going to happen to me? Will I swing by a rope ending this charade or will justice be done, and I will walk free?" These thought coursed through her mind as she sat in solitary confinement waiting for the verdict of the Court.

Thinking back on the matter she tried to explain to herself how she arrived in this awful circumstance. Life had been so perfect, so beautiful. She could not understand why everything was being taken away from her.

She thought back to the first day of the trial. They brought her into court with a bag on her head. She could hardly breathe. Her clothing stunk from wearing it for the last two weeks. There was no bath, no soap, no visitors, and just constant questions. Whatever she said did not please her interrogators.

"Who are your accomplices?"

"I have no accomplices. I don't understand why I am here. What have I done? Why are you treating me like this?"

"You better give us the information we want, it will go easier on you!"

"What information do you want, what is it you want me to say?"

That brought a sharp slap to her face. She could feel the sting of her interrogator's ring as it ripped her cheekbone.

"Don't fuck with us; you know exactly what information we want. You can do this the easy way or the hard way. We have all the time in the world."

Suddenly her arms were tied together and she was pulled up on a rope suspended from the ceiling. She felt herself twirling round and round, spinning like a top. She was frightened and did not know what to do.

She began to cry out because she felt like her arms were going to pull out of her shoulder sockets. When she started to cry she felt the sting of the whip. At first her pants protected her butt and legs, but the interrogator quickly ripped off her outer clothing, and now she could really feel the sting of the whip.

She could not look down but it felt as if there were deep red welts appearing on her torso and butt. One snap of the whip caught her in the groin. They say a woman is not sensitive in the groin like a man. That's a crock of shit. She never felt such pain in her life.

She could tell her interrogator seemed to take a perverse delight in the whipping. She seemed to enjoy inflicting pain. The more Jocelyn cried out the harder the blows. It felt like she was hanging there for hours. The reality was that it only lasted for 30 minutes.

Jocelyn passed out and later found herself lying on the concrete floor of her cell. There was blood all over and she had peed and shit her underwear. She hurt all over and was disgusted with herself.

She crawled up to the stainless steel toilet and tried to wash off the grime of the day. She stood there over the toilet without benefit of any body cover. She washed her clothes as clean as she could and then sat on the concrete floor with her head between her legs sobbing to herself.

The door to her cell began to open. It was as if two giant pieces of steel were cranking by each other. Two men and a woman were standing there. She recognized the woman as her tormentor. The men were just there as muscle. Fear began to etch in her throat and she felt herself begin to tremble.

"Are you ready to confess?"

She felt her lips slowly moving. She had to be very careful. In a faint voice she said, "Confess to what?"

"You know!"

Jocelyn did not like her tone and instantly suspected she was going to start beating her again. Instinctively she raised her hand to her head in a protective motion. She need not have bothered.

The two men walked over to her and each grabbed an arm and led her away. She began to fear her end was coming. She did not understand how much pain the body could take before it longed for the peace of the grave. They took her into a small room with a wooden chair with straps for her arms, legs and core. She couldn't resist them. Her strength was gone and even if she had strength, she recognized she was not a match for two of them. Before they strapped her in the chair they cut off her underpants. She began to really worry. She noticed that the chair had an odd depression in the seat and wondered what its purpose was. She felt her legs pulled apart with her genitalia completely exposed. One of the guards rolled over a machine with electrodes. There was an electrode on the end of each cable, and the machine was plugged into a wall socket. He quickly reached under her into her crotch and attached the electrode to the area of her clitoris.

Jocelyn's apprehension was enormous. She could feel her heart begin to beat at an accelerated pace and it felt like the top of her head was going to come off. She had heard of this being done to men, but never to women. She felt that every part of her body had been violated. The worst was yet to come.

"Are you ready to confess?"

Jocelyn tried to gain time and reason with her. "What shall I confess to? What do you want me to say?"

Her interrogator was not amused by her comment. She nodded to the male guard and in an instant Jocelyn felt the jolt of the electrical current to her privates. Most men think the clitoris is just a little button. They are so-oo wrong. The clitoris is a major organ that extends around the vagina. She felt her whole organ shake in pain.

It was not the eruption of an organism; it was the infliction of terrible pain. It seemed to last forever. Sometimes pain is so bad that the victim simply suffers in silence. She felt herself beginning to withdraw. She retreated into a small corner of her mind where none of this was happening. She heard her ask again.

"Are you ready to confess?"

Jocelyn did not answer. She had found a safe haven. Again the electricity coursed through her body but with greater intensity. The scene repeated itself for the next two hours. She woke up two days later in her cell. She found a dry piece of bread with cold peas in a bowl. There was no spoon. She eagerly ate the bread and peas with her hands. She licked the bowl to taste the last drop of salt.

There was a stainless steel mirror on the wall. It did not give the best reflection, but what she saw was enough. Starring back at her was a puffy faced creature with blood shot eyes, scraggly hair and a swollen face. She did not recognize herself. She starred for a long time and began to recognize how far from grace she had fallen. She could not understand what had happened to her. After all, she was not a genetic defective that was fed to the Legionnaires. Her gene splice was perfect or as close to perfect as could possibly exist. What was she doing here? Why was she being punished? What was her crime?

There was no food or water for the next two days. She began to experience diarrhea and could not control her bowels. The problem was that nothing went in and nothing came out. She just had the worst cramps, pain and gas imaginable.

On the third day, they returned.

She could feel that her spirit was broken. Her journey had come to an end. She recognized that you can break any person. That without a support system any person will collapse and withdraw. She would give them whatever they wanted. She simply wanted the peace of the grave. No more pain.

"Are you ready to confess?"

"Yes, tell me what you want me to say. I will do anything."

Chapter 25

Jocelyn Jones

In the 21ˢᵗ Century, American values had a unique component that was seldom found in other cultures.

The values held by the vast majority of Americans were branded by the great tradition of the English common law.

Two great concepts were ingrained in the psyche of most Americans.

Tolerance of divergent viewpoints manifested itself through the First Amendment to the Constitution. People were free to speak their beliefs regardless of whether such beliefs and values conflicted with their neighbor. Free speech was only limited by incitement. This was a rational extrapolation designed to balance the right to speak out on any issue against the potential to destroy the social fabric of the country.

Along with freedom of speech came an abiding respect for the rights of the individual.

The courts of the country long recognized that the individual was powerless to act when confronted by the awesome power of the state. Safeguards were put in place to protect the individual from arbitrary punitive state action. These rights included the right to a fair trial, the right to confront and Cross examine your accusers, the right to the effective assistance of counsel and most importantly the right to test by constitutional question the imposition of laws and sanctions that impinged directly on the individual.

Life in the 51ˢᵗ Century was quite different. Laws were no longer promulgated by a legislature elected by the people. The courts had ceased to function 100 years after the Great War. After a time, the concept of a lawyer as an advocate who protected the rights of the individual from arbitrary state action faded from view. All that mattered was the survival of the nation state. After all, what need was there for courts when loyalty was pledged to the Secretariat. The rules of life were clear.

Genetic selection was producing the desired traits in individuals and those who were rejects simply found their way into the Legion or the many brothels that served the Legion.

Trial by a jury of one's peers was an oxymoron concept. One's peers could only be those within the same genetic line and disobedience to objective was not an option. In the quest for national survival the American values that distinguished American life from all other cultures had been lost.

Jocelyn was puzzled. What was it that brought about her fall from grace? Looking backward she realized there had been an extraordinary level of killing during the 21st Century. The conflict had persisted for 3,000 years. The conflict was a foul odor that pervaded every aspect of 51st Century life. Genetic selection had derailed the moral climate of the country. The arts, the rule of law, and respect for the rights of the individual were no longer relevant to daily life.

Jocelyn could not fathom her situation. She was a member of the political elite. What crime of treachery had she committed that would drag her to this low point in life? Why was the very essence of life being ripped from her body? What act of treachery could justify what was being done to her? She did not conceive of herself as a political person; she was certainly not a revolutionary and did not seek the overthrow of the Secretariat. It was the farthest thought from her mind.

They dragged her into the dark room. She was shackled to a chair with bright white lights shinning directly into her face. It was difficult to make out the images in front of her. To her right and left stood a Legionnaire. She thought she could make out three people sitting on a raised dais directly in front of her. There was a deathly silence in the room. She sat and waited for someone to speak. Fear pervaded every part of her body. It was the unknown. She could not accept what fate had in store for her.

In 21st Century America there was a concept often called due process. Very few could precisely define what it meant. Meaning was dependent on a case by case basis. In its most elemental form, due process suggested there had to be some fundamental fairness when the power of the state was brought to bear against the individual. Due process as a concept did not exist in Jocelyn's world. She had never heard of the concept, let alone the words. Nonetheless she felt there was something very unfair about what was going to happen to her.

As she waited in silence, a flood of thoughts crept through her mind. She thought about her casual encounter with Gaul and their subsequent meeting. She knew he was very powerful, but she was not particularly attracted to him. Besides, she thought, he was probably doing some young girl. What would he want with a 46 year old woman? Her own thoughts confused her. She was in a good relationship with Leslie but always wondered in the corner of her mind if Leslie cherished her or simply remained with her because of her power and influence?

What would Leslie think now? Would she come to see her in this condition or would she simply pass by on the street as if they were complete strangers? She wondered if a man would do the same thing? Do men make lasting commitments or are their relationships simply transitory and a function of power and influence? More than that is it fair to make such sweeping generalizations? These thoughts recycled through her mind as she waited for sound to emerge in the room.

"Jocelyn Jones, you are charged with high treason during a time of war! Do you admit your treacherous conduct?"

She sat stunned by the allegation. She had no contact with the enemy, and had never had a treasonous thought in her mind. Her thoughts were primarily about how well the Secretariat ran the country and how she could sustain the relationship with her lover. She was essentially intelligent but did not know what question to formulate in response to the issue that was put to her. A few moments of silence went by.

Finally she blurted out, "What act of treason am I accused of? What is it that I have done? I do not understand?"

She heard her three tormentors talking among themselves. She could not make out what they were saying, but from the tone of it, she recognized things did not bode well for her.

"Remove her! We have no more time to waste with characters of this ilk. When she is ready to confess her sins, escort her back to this chamber."

Her restraints were quickly removed and she was escorted to a new room of horrors. In this new chamber she would feel the pain that comes with affliction of the body. They began by pulling out her nails from her feet. They started with the big toe on her right foot. She was unable to balance and fell to the ground. The pain was unbearable. She never knew she had so many nerve endings in one toe.

"Do you confess?"

"Yes, yes, I am guilty!"

"What are you guilty of? What is it that you did?"

Jocelyn was blank. She did not understand. She blurted out, "I don't know what I did."

They moved to the big toe on the left foot. Jocelyn thought that the previous pain could not be duplicated. She was wrong. All she could see was blood at her feet. She could not walk or stand. She hobbled about on her knees much the way a dog would walk. The questioning began again, but by now she was too exhausted to respond. Her interrogators knew that the session was done for the day.

It has been said there is no limit to human depravity. As if to inflict the last drop of pain to her psyche, the lead interrogator said, "By the way, your little trollup is dead." Jocelyn began to moan. She could not contain herself any longer. Why Leslie? What had she done to anyone? She was just a sweet stupid girl of 25. She had hardly lived. To hear that her life was snuffed out made no sense. What danger was she to anyone? Jocelyn's world had turned upside down. In the space of a few days all of the perceptions that she believed to be true were undercut and discarded. She found herself on a lonely journey to damnation.

Chapter 26

Gaul

Gaul had become quite adept at his searches in the Las Vegas Public Library. He reasoned that there must be other libraries in the old cities. In the back of his mind he wondered if there was some central Library where all information was stored in one computer. What a find that would be.

He did not consider the political implications of his actions nor did he give a thought to their consequences. He felt simply driven by the quest to know.

In that sense he was like every other man, since we climbed down from the trees and started walking upright on the earth.

He began to spend more and more of his time at the Library and soon set up a cool room and security breaks. The last thing he wanted was to be discovered. When he felt ready, he would reveal his knowledge to the Committee of the Inner Circle. For now this was his secret.

What he did not know was that there was an Inner Circle within the Inner Circle and that through each generation the secrets of the 21st Century had been handed down to each Chairman as a sacred trust. When in the lifetime of some remote Chairman, the Chairman felt it was time to reveal all, such would be done.

In the meantime in 3,000 years of succession the secret remained inviolate. The truth was found in the old adage, Power Corrupts and absolute power Corrupts Absolutely.

By their nature men do not willing surrender power. Chairman Warden was not about to give up her iron grip on America. She actually believed that what she was doing was for the common good and to protect the security of the state.

It was not a matter of delusion. Her beliefs were firmly rooted in 3,000 years of history and progress as she and those of the Inner Circle defined progress. Catastrophic war had been eliminated. Disease was eliminated. There was no hunger and the life span of useful units had been increased to 150 years. What more could anyone want? This was an idealic society, free of major war and famine. Everyone was happy.

Social defectives were removed through the use of the Legion and its brothels. What more could any society strive for?

Occasionally she was puzzled by use of the term "In God We Trust," but by and large her life was satisfactory. Gunter Ras liked to suck up to the old lady. He could never see her in a sexual context, but if he had to he would do her if it would advance his career. Luckily for him he was not called on to perform. His contact with her was limited to being her faithful retainer and gopher. This did not bother him. He did not mind that other people in government referred to him as her butt boy. He actually enjoyed knowing that others were jealous of his association with Chairman Warden.

He would occasionally become upset when he heard talk that he was her lover. He always felt above her, and besides who could stand such a rational mind as Warden's. She was too detached from ordinary people to be interesting.

The thought of a sexual relationship with her was repulsive to him. Powerful women intrigued him, and their strength inured to his benefit.

Chapter 27

Attack on the Citadel

Gaul was acutely aware of the nature of history. He recognized that every step he took would be judged in the full measure of time for many generations to come.

At 46 he was a measured man, seasoned in the ways of life, yet still in his prime. He now considered the full measure of what had been and what had become of the United States. Measured by the objective standards of history, the United States had degraded to the equivalent of a medieval fife where the cause of liberty was non-existent and humanity was sacrificed on the alter of the state.

In youth many men have illusions of self-importance. There is a keen desire to change the world to reflect the man's idea of what is good. Good is a subjective term, typically defined as what is good for the leader. Gaul was amused by these thoughts because his objective was much loftier. If he failed in his mission, death would be painful and protracted. There would be no swift shot to the head that would end his criminal enterprise. If he succeeded, children for many generations would recite his name in their evening prayers and long after his bones had turned to dust he would be recalled with reverence and respect. Such are the things of men.

The decision to attack the Citadel was not an intellectual exercise in good and evil. It simply rested on the premise that all men die at some point in time. Death is the inevitable conclusion of life. It is how you live and place your life at risk to death that really matters.

An empty life without challenge is no life at all. Granted that at some point in time we all seek a certain peaceful oblivion. Gaul was not cut from this placid bolt of cloth. His was the world of direct action where all was won or lost in the burst of a Remington Blast Rifle. It was not a world of chivalry. He was fond of the expression "Chivalry is dead, long live the Secretary." Gaul recognized that the world was at a turning point. Either it gradually returned to what was good in the 21st Century, or it would spin out of control and mankind would be one more endangered species. His view had evolved in a worldly conception of man's role, if any, in the universe. He was always asking himself, "Who is this upright creature that walks on two legs and seeks to dominate all sentient life?"

Of course he had no cut and dried answer and could only rummage though the philosophy books in the Library looking for a gateway to the answer.

Gaul was discouraged by the attitude of the Secretariat. What disturbed him the most was the caviler manner in which life was treated. Unbeknown to Secretary Warden, life is a precious commodity if it is to maintain its value. To maintain value, life must be venerated. Every person must be deemed to have a quality that transcends the person.

For two years Gaul had been carefully building his battle plan. Recognizing there was only one opportunity for victory, he carefully crafted his ideas, and surrounded himself with officers whose personal loyalty to him was unquestioned.

He wanted to be certain that in the course of the attack there would be no dual loyalties or defections from his command. In selecting his people there were two concerns. First, he expected his staff to have high intellect. He did not want any yes men. He did not seek to have his ultimate battle plan challenged, but did seek out officers who would challenge his tactical moves.

Only in officers who had the confidence to question the feasibility of tactics did he feel some assurance of favorable outcome. He was dismissive of officers on the general staff. They were old, puffy and unimaginative. He sought out the vibrancy of the young colonels who were not merely putting in their time with the expectation of collecting their pension.

He had no illusion that these men were fighting for freedom and Republican government. It would take total re-education and years of idea exchange to make Democrats out of this bunch. What was required now was personal loyalty, military brilliance and a lot of luck.

No city had been attacked from the air for over 3,000 years. Military doctrine considered it a war crime to bomb from the air because of collateral damage and the inability to distinguish civilians from combatants. Weapons of mass destruction were likewise outlawed under the present rules of engagement.

The necessity for these rules became manifest following the American response to the initial Islamic attack. Both sides recognized the necessity for selfrestraint because a failure to exercise such restraint would result in total destruction. That is not to say that war games ceased to be played or that air and missile forces went out of business. To the contrary, research and development continued and each side attempted to gain a leg up on the other with the hope that the scientific research would produce the silver bullet.

Gaul fashioned a plan to attack the Citadel from the air, and at the same time launch a ground offensive that was designed to penetrate the defenses of the city. He knew that the air attack was doomed to failure and that corpses of those who participated would be just so much dust in the wind in the hours following the air attack.

As a tactician he knew that it was necessary to launch the air attack and that it would fail. It was designed to fail and mislead. That was a part of his plan. Here he was required to exert duplicity. His motives must not become transparent.

He summoned Colonel Bird Oliver of the 55th Tactical Air Wing Command. Bird Oliver was happy to be in the shadow of Gaul. He had always suspected that Gaul had something to do with advancing his career.

At a gut level he understood that there was little to distinguish one Lieutenant Colonel from another, and that at his level of rank, unless someone smiled on him from above, the chance of further promotion was non-existent.

Bird appeared at Gaul's office 30 minutes before their scheduled meeting. His nervousness and anticipation was apparent to Master Sergeant Gloria Barnes. After identifying himself she turned back to her computer and refused to engage in any polite chit chat. Oliver sat in ramrod silence with a small tick in his right eye that gave away his apprehension. One minute after the appointed time of the meeting he was ushered into Gaul's office.

"Colonel, so nice to see you."

"Thank you sir for having me come in."

"I want to visit with you today about something of national interest. Naturally I expect your total silence and complete discretion."

Bird could hardly believe what he was hearing. This was his big day. This was his opportunity to reveal his loyalty to Gaul. This was his chance to prove the excellence of his performance and get ahead of the pack. He was all ears. He would do what was asked of him without question. Whatever it took he would demonstrate his loyalty.

Gaul had been very careful in his selection of Bird. He chose him because he had no extended social contacts. He was known to have many lovers, but had no one living with him on a permanent basis. He was a clear thinker who was well respected by the men, but close to no one. He would be remembered by a few and missed by none should he perish in the operation. A good oration and military funeral would accompany him on his way.

"Bird, there have been rumors of a conspiracy to topple the government. I don't know what you've heard but the rumors are true."

Bird's eyes opened wide with anticipation. Gaul could sense that he had captured his full attention.

"The rumors are true and false."

Bird reeled back not certain he understood what he was hearing. How could such a rumor be true and false in the same context?

"You see, what has happened is that the Secretariat has sought to dissolve the Council and seize absolute power." Bird had never been interested in politics but instantly feared that such a move would personally impact him in a negative way. You don't get to be a colonel without some savvy of how the game is played.

"We have to act to protect our American way of life."

Bird was not sure what this meant, but he knew that if he elected not to be a player he would be short lived. A decision point was upon him.

Nodding his head in assent he joined the conspiracy. He understood he would be called on to carry out his duty. He believed that no matter what the cost of the duty, he would personally survive and prosper.

Chapter 28

Attack on the Citadel 2

A successful military campaign requires meticulous planning. Even if all of the planning is perfect the organizer of the event must be prepared for rapid changes on the ground that will alter the plan. The plan is a mere conception; the actual battle rarely if ever mimics the plan.

Gaul was familiar with all of the classic historical campaigns. He was the consummate military historian. He recognized that wars were not won by swordsmanship and feats of bravado. Battles were won or lost by the massive application of force and adherence to objective.

He knew that in Gunter Ras he faced a clever and ruthless adversary. Gunter was after all the boot boy of Chairman Warden. He knew that his fate was inexorably tied to her continued well being. That without her he would simply fade into obscurity. He was fond of MacArthur's expression that, "Old soldiers never die, they just fade away." He had no intention of fading away.

He was intelligent enough to know that he could never supplant the Chairman, but as the mace in her hand he wielded unbridled power. He did not intend to lose that power.

As a Colonel General in the Legion, Gaul had unbridled access to all of the psychological files of its members. He intended to use his intelligence advantage in the coming uprising.

He carefully examined the Psych Department's evaluation of Gunter. He looked for chinks in his armor that could be used to advantage in the upcoming battle. On the surface he did not see any apparent weaknesses in his adversary. Putting the file down on his desk, he leaned back in his chair considering the information on Gunter Ras.

While the man had no apparent weakness, he lacked one key element in his personality. Gunter's personality profile was a straight line. He lacked the capacity of flexibility. He could not turn in the wind and alter his objective to changed conditions on the ground. He had one gear in his head: Forward! There was no room to turn to the right or left depending on changes in the situation on the ground. He could be counted on to fight to the death, even his own death because that was his nature. Survival was not an object in his makeup if it was contrary to his plan.

In a sense he had adopted the philosophy of the Spartan Greeks. "Come home victorious or on your shield." That is not a good philosophy for a militarist. Gaul wondered how to turn the personality to his advantage.

The Legion was an army that had grown soft. It had sat in preparation for global warfare for 3,000 years. True it engaged in small skirmishes; however it must be remembered that small skirmishes are not the substance of global warfare. It is one thing to visualize a few men dead on a battlefield. It is quite something else to envision the carnage of a Stalingrad where tens of thousands rot in the frozen waters of the Volga River. This is what destroys the minds of men, because it brings home how insignificant each soldier is. A mere tooth on a cog of one of the many instruments of war.

It is the adjustment of a man's mind to such insignificance that is the harm. It is not the smell of cordite, or the sight of eviscerated bodies that brings horror to the mind. It is the recognition of the insignificance of the individual that causes the damage to the psyche of a man. The Legion was not prepared for this kind of warfare.

Gaul combed through the archives of the architectural plan of the Citadel. So many years and modifications. It had grown as a hive; however the centrality of its core had not changed. All command and control operations were safely nestled in the core of the hive. On paper it appeared impregnable.

Then it occurred to Gaul there was an inherent weakness in the design. The core did not contain its own power source. Such a source would have been impossible to maintain so far underground. It depended for its power on a series of lightly fortified stations. True it could hold out on internal batteries for seven days, but beyond that it would simply become an engineered coffin sitting deep in the neck of the mountain.

A plan began to take shape in Gaul's mind. He was concerned that the eastern block might use any attack on the Citadel as an excuse to initiate its own mischief. That event had to be avoided at all costs.

He feared that the north and south post of the Legion would remain loyal to the Chairman and that his troops would be caught in a pincer movement when Gunter Ras' forces advanced. A frontal assault was not the choice of operational plans. Instead he formulated a plan for an all out air attack where all forces would be concentrated on repulsing the incoming flights of aero attackers.

The attackers could not appear to come from their base to the southwest of the Citadel. The attack would have to launch from the east so as to simulate an attack from the eastern block. For this he would have Bird Oliver position 300 of his best attack aircraft at bases in what was once Florida and South Carolina. The planes would be slowly moved to these bases for repair and only returned to ready duty on paper. They would become a phantom force, sitting in readiness for the appointed date.

Gaul had become something of a student of history and wanted to commence the rebellion on the 4th of July. He saw a symbolism in this date that would not be lost on later generations. Unfortunately the arrest of Jocelyn Jones necessitated that the date of rebellion be advanced to May 1st. If the Chairman and her henchmen discerned his relationship with Jocelyn, it might well be another 10,000 years before there would be another chance for rebellion. He had to move fast. Time was not on his side.

Chapter 29

Attack on the Prison

Jocelyn's arrest had come as a shock to Gaul. When he left the pamphlet in her apartment he never considered that any peering eyes would discover it. For the first time in his life he felt a sense of guilt.

It troubled him that Leslie had been beaten to death by Gunter Ras and his thugs. There were no real secrets in the Citadel. As soon as she was dead word leaked back to Gaul. And now Jocelyn.

He carefully considered his plans. Should he advance the date of the attack to save Jocelyn with the possible failure of the revolution in the balance? It deeply troubled him. Sleep would not come. In his mind he could see the degradation she would undergo. He vicariously felt her pain and anxiety. Moreover she did not know why she was being accused. Unless she had read Paine's ideas, she would never be able to give them what they wanted.

In a nanosecond he realized that this woman was very important to him. Something in her had awakened a restless spirit deep within his consciousness. How could that be? He mulled it over and over in his mind, but could not articulate a rational explanation.

Gaul summoned all of his lieutenants.

"Gentlemen, I had planned the attack on the Citadel to commence on July 4th. There is a certain symbolism involved in starting the revolution on that day. Unfortunately we have to move the day up. We will attack 24 hours from now on May 1st."

A hushed silence fell over the room. Men looked around with strange thoughts in their heads. Collectively they realized that many of them would not survive the attack. The moment of self-realization that death was around the corner sent an eerie feeling into the room. It was not fear. It was the realization that many universes would soon cease to exist. Mortality is a strange phenomenon.

"You have the plans for the coordinated air offensive. At 0100 hours I expect the air attack to begin. There are going to be losses. I expect the attack to be pressed regardless of losses. In theory all of your flying to this date has been a rehearsal for this one event. This is main stage."

Gaul did not tell them that the air attack was merely a ruse and that he anticipated there would be 100 percent losses. He could not tell them. The airmans' destiny was to lead the armada of force against the Citadel while the real attack took place deep within its bowels.

These airmen would be sacrificed for the good of the revolution and future of the country. They would be remembered and their names would be venerated. Perhaps even a school would be named after one or more of them, assuming a return to Republican government. That was off in the distant future.

For now he needed the attack to create a diversion. His real intent was to save Jocelyn. He recognized that this was not the best way to restart the country. The good of the country comes first, but he was a man.

When a man falls in love with a woman he is a crazy animal. He had fallen in love with Jocelyn Jones and would not allow anyone to stand in his way. If it meant the sacrifice of 2,000 airmen it was of little concern to him. All he could think of was that he gave everything for the good of the revolution, and he would not allow anyone to take away his little piece of happiness.

The air attack began. At once the night sky was punctuated with the smell of aviation gas. Against the Ark of the Citadel there was a background of massive bolts of high energy blast rifles waiting to erupt. The attackers were good. They held their formation and continued on in a relentless manner. The antiaircraft crews were better. They did not depend on the soul of a man to fire.

Deep in the core of the Citadel computers targeted multiple aircraft as they came in for the attack. When the particle beams from their blast rifles struck any part of the aircraft there was a sizzle followed by an explosion. The Citadel had planned for this attack for 3,000 years. Gaul's lieutenants had planned their attack for 7 days. He watched on his computer as the planes came in. As they were hit they disappeared from the screen.

One weapons officer managed to eject from his crippled aircraft. He was horribly burned. Troops loyal to the Secretary paraded him before the television. His face and hands were not recognizable. He had the appearance of a crispy critter. His condition was of little note. What was important was the diversion.

Gaul's men had managed to pin down desperate elements of the Legion stationed in the surrounding base areas.

He knew he had to lead the raiding party to free Jocelyn. The thought preoccupied and pervaded his mind. He was not suspect in any part of the attack. In fact Chairman Warden considered him to be a loyal retainer.

Gaul and seven of his men slipped into the elevator. They were heavily armed. This did not arouse any suspicion because there were armed men everywhere. After all, the Citadel was under attack.

They dropped 1500 feet to the level of the prison cells. A surprised sergeant rose quickly to his feet to salute Gaul. He was cut down before he was three quarters of the way up. He died silently. Prison guards tended to be a lazy lot. They were certainly not the front line troops of the Legion.

As they passed from the outer entrance to the cells the group of 7 fanned out. As soon as they saw someone that was not part of the group, they killed him without mercy. Their orders were to take no prisoners. This was not an intelligence gathering mission. This was a mission to save the life of Jocelyn.

For the most part the cells were empty. Gaul flung open the door to Jocelyn's cell. At first she did not understand what was happening. She thought this was the end. They had come for her. With all the dignity she could muster she rose to her feet and looked squarely at Gaul. Their eyes met and locked in a mental embrace. He walked to her and took her in his arms. He could feel her body shivering.

"I love you so much."

She heard the words over and over in her mind. She did not understand. She knew that he had rescued her but for what purpose. She felt herself fold into his arms and begin to sob in deep emotion.

Grasping his chest she pulled herself into him. He quickly covered her with a cloak.

"Come, we have to move quickly. We cannot linger here. It's too dangerous."

At ground lever the battle continued. The air assault was failing. The streets of the Citadel were littered with broken parts from the composite material of the downed airships. Here and there a burned corpse was visible with the agony of the last moment of life etched in the face of the deceased. It was not pretty. In a few days it would smell like the refuse of the garbage dump.

"Jocelyn, I have to leave you here. You will be safe. I'm leaving my seven best men to guard you. I have to lead the attack. There is so little time. I don't want to leave you, but this is our only chance. Do you understand?"

She began to shake again. Clinging to Gaul she begged him not to go. In her mind there was no clarity as to future events. Her reality was the safety of this little anonymous room. It was obscure and opaque to all eyes.

Her voice was barely a whisper.

"Promise me that you will come back. Promise me!"

Gaul held her face in his hands. He kissed her closed eye lids and ran his tongue over her nose and cheeks. With that he turned and walked away to finish the blood business of the night.

Chapter 30

Battle for Control of the Citadel

Chairman Warden rested comfortably in her bunker in the Citadel. The attack was being repulsed without loss on the side of the Secretariat. It had been a furious battle. All of the attacking aeros had been destroyed. Gunter Ras was at her side.

"I'm very pleased with the way you have handled the defense of the Citadel. It's a testament to your command."

From one of the few captured airman she learned that Gaul was at the head of the revolt.

"When I get through with General Gaul, you can have him to do as you will. I assure you there won't be much left, but he may provide you some amusement."

Gunter liked to be stroked. It enhanced his image of himself and importance in the eyes of the Chairman. In point of fact the destruction of the raiders in the aero attack had nothing to do with his leadership. The defensive weapons of the Citadel had been preprogrammed for hundreds of years. Its concentric fire zones were the product of engineers who had long since passed. All that Gunter's troops did was to monitor the computers that controlled the antiaircraft blast artillery. It was not very imaginative work. On the other hand he fancied himself to be a leader of men, and it flattered his vanity to the point where he actually believed he had saved the Citadel.

It never occurred to him that the aero attack was a ruse to divert his attention from an eminent ground seizure. He basked in the immediate adulation and glory of the sacrifice of the aero squadrons. He was not a real soldier. He wore the uniform of a soldier, and acted with the authority of command, but his at core he was no more than a thespian on the stage.

Ask any man who has every served in a rifle company and he will tell you that a real officer is one who leads by example. A real officer says "Follow me," and advances into the thicket of the fray. It is not a matter of being fearless to the injury and death of combat. It is a love of conflict and the primitive force that compels men to compete in combat's dance to death. A real officer has integrity. He eats what his men eat, and shares the same ground in slumber. There is no double standard for officers and men. Men follow him because he sets the example. He does not sit behind a rock at the base of the hill and order his men to advance up the hill in the face of withering fire. He advances at the head of his men. Gunter Ras was not this kind of officer. When others were hard in training, he was looking at himself in the mirror, fancying what a handsome image he made.

Gaul had studied all of the maps of the Citadel. He had been in the Chairman's bunker on many occasions. Over the last two years he had carefully mapped all of the escape tunnels, entrances and exits to the bunker. He no longer needed to look at a map to know his location.

He believed that if he cut off the head of government the revolution had a chance of success. He did not want a prolonged civil war. Such a war would rip the country apart, and beside that there was no longer an ideological thread of difference between the sides. He was the one that must spark the ideological difference, and this could only occur if he was able to capture the Chairman and her cronies.

With utmost care he selected the Legionnaires who were to block the tunnels leading to the entrances and exits of the Chairman's bunker. They were not chosen for their intellect or their belief in the rights of the common man. They were chosen because they could be counted on to fight to the death in loyalty to Gaul. They were the best of their kind. They were certainly not Republicans, but they knew their station in life and were determined to exercise their loyalty to Gaul no matter what the cost.

At the appointed hour the attack on the bunker began. Gaul's men simultaneously appeared at the entrance of each tunnel. Everything appeared normal to the defenders. Without entering the chamber at the end of each tunnel, Gaul's men flooded the chamber with phosphorous and fragmentation grenades. The result was devastating. In a few minutes what remained of the mangled corpses of the defenders rested where they died, many still in flame from the burning phosphorous. In a contained room where the walls are reinforced and there is nowhere to run this was a horrible fate. The beauty of the attack was that it was simultaneous, unanticipated by the defenders and merciless.

Gaul burst into the bunker of the Chairman to the amazement of Gunter Ras. The occupants of the bunker were quickly subdued and disarmed. Actually they offered little resistance. They displayed shock at the turn of events. It was inconceivable how this turn of events could have come about. The Chairman was protesting to one of the Legionaries.

"I am Chairman Warden. You are acting illegally. Release me at once. You have no authority to do what you've done. You'll all be executed as traitors."

Gaul's men paid little heed to her. They searched her for weapons and restrained her arms. One of the men pulled a black hood over her head and led her away with the others.

"Make sure she is not harmed. That goes for the others too! I don't care what threats she makes. Treat her with respect and lock her up. If we don't do this right there will be a total blood bath the likes of which have never been seen before. Understood?"

"Yes Sir."

Gaul knew his orders would be followed. For now he had to secure the Citadel against the inevitable counter attack.

Chapter 31

Moses

Gaul had read the Old Testament. He was particularly fascinated with the Book of Exodus. In many ways it exemplified the difficult problems he faced.

According to the history, when Moses led the Children of Israel out of Egypt they wandered for 40 years in the desert without coming to the Promised Land. There were many scholarly arguments advanced as to why it took so long to enter Israel.

For Gaul there was only one that made sense. You cannot build a nation of slaves. Slaves will always be slaves. A man has to taste the sweet breath of freedom. When he does he will fight to protect that freedom. The same analogy was true with regard to the revolt. It was inconceivable that he could build a nation out of the remnants of the Legion and the technocrats that supported the Secretariat.

A new generation would have to take their place. A generation that was taught to think, that knew its history, and which was irreverent to authority.

In his mind he saw the new American. He was very much like the Americans of old who threw off the yoke of European authority derived through bloodlines, in favor of an egalitarian view of the world. It would be a tough road. The end would not come in Gaul's lifetime. He would try and set the stage, but the play was yet to be written.

Chapter 32

A Sense of Justice

"We have to bring these people to trial. They have done immeasurable harm to the body politic."

With that Gaul sat down. He had made his case for the sedition trial of Secretary Warden, Gunter Ras and the various henchmen who served the cause of the Secretariat.

Very few in attendance understood the concept of harm to the body politic. What they saw was a Colonel General of the Legion who now held absolute power. The words meant nothing to most in attendance. What meant something was the directive he was trending toward. All present assumed this was the mandate of the time.

A tall thin man with pitch black hair stood up as Gaul sat down. "You don't understand. I agree with you that there has to be some kind of trial, but what are the charges? There has not been a lawyer in this country for over 3,000 years. We have no system of rules for our revolution to correct the wrongs committed by the Secretariat. Do we get to make the rules? Is that the right of the victor?"

Gaul recognized that a smart man was speaking. He now saw problems that had not occurred to him. His initial reaction following the revolution and incarceration of the Secretary was to have a quick trial and force the Secretary and her followers to plead their own cases. It now occurred to him that this would not work because it would appear that due process was being denied the loser. He did not want the trial to be a drum head court's martial where the guilt of the Secretariat was already determined and the trial was merely a showpiece to instill fear in the body politic.

The tall man went on.

"We have to create a system of law that provides equal justice for all, regardless of the heinous nature of the crimes that are charged. At the end of the day, it must appear that the accused was given a fair trial and an opportunity to dispel the charges against her. This means the accused has to have a lawyer who understands the principles of the law and the rules of evidence."

With that he was silent.

Gaul found himself again addressing the assembly. He had to think on his feet or all would be lost.

"I believe that Evan is right. He has obviously taken advantage of the Library and has been digging into our history. I propose that Evan be granted the status of Dean, and that he find 20 of the brightest young minds to study every aspect of the law. That we give him 5 years to complete his assignment. From these twenty, five shall be judges, five shall be advocates and ten shall be teachers. We have to foster a system of rules that sanctions conduct that is inherently wrong or morally offensive. I don't know where we are going with this, but I do know that we can keep the Secretary and her followers locked up for the next five year until our feet are grounded in a system that is prepared to meet out justice. There has to be transparency. The rules have to be fair. I like things that are exact, but that is a criticism of my background. I was brought up as a militarist. We have to return to our roots. Militarism and autocratic government are a dead-end. Both lack a moral direction. We have to return to democracy. From what I have read, democracy is not orderly. It is messy. There are many personal choices to make. We will stumble along the way but the road ahead is clear. I also propose that we undertake a program to educate our brightest young people and expose them to the great books in the Library."

The words came out effortlessly. Gaul understood there was a vast difference between words and action. Words are powerful elements that can spur people to action, however recorded history evidences many dictators who promise much with their words and only exercise unbridled self-interest. This time it must be different. He thought to himself, for once it must be different. He was mindful from his reading of the history of Mexico. There was always a revolution in Mexico, but once the revolutionaries got into power they betrayed the revolution. He would not allow this to happen.

Gaul's words for now had the force of law. Even though Gaul was in power, the reeducation of America had not taken place. There was no dissent. What he mandated as a matter of principal took place. The face of the nation would radically change over the next five years. It would never be as it was now. The test of its future would lay in the fairness of the trial of the Secretary and her followers. America was about to experience the joy of free speech.

Chapter 33

The Trial

Five years had passed since revolutionary eve. Much had changed in the life of the average American. Gaul's days seemed to be filled from morning till late every evening with the affairs of state. He did not seek to micro manage the lives of his fellow Americans but sought to put in place a series of Czars who would reestablish democratic institutions and Republican government. There had not been a 3rd Estate for 3,000 years. He wondered how you create a free press in a society that simply accepted authority without question. It deeply troubled him. Secretary Warden, Gunter Ras and their henchmen had been safely locked up in maximum security for five years. Their lives were easy and routine.

Gaul found himself in constant conflict with Jocelyn. She demanded more and more of his time. He wanted to give her what she demanded but the affairs of government always seemed to interfere in their daily life. So much had changed in their personal lives.

When Gaul took Jocelyn she was 46 and had never used any birth control device. She had never been with a man. He was her first and only man. A few months later to her immediate chagrin she found herself pregnant with child. She was horrified. Children were always bred in the bionics laboratory. There had not been a real birth, to her knowledge, in 3,000 years. She had no concept of prenatal care and did not know what to do. A kind of negative panic set in where she was mentally immobilized. In her 4th month Gaul noticed the subtle changes that were taking place in her body. Her face was always flushed and seemed to take on a beautiful reddish color. At first he refused to accept that this event could be happening, and realized that they had to talk. It was awkward because in past times it was the woman who announced the coming event. Jocelyn did not know how to articulate her situation.

"I think something special is happening between us," Gaul said.

She looked up at him quizzically and nodded in agreement. "So, when did you have your last period?"

No one had ever asked her this before. She was flustered by this seeming invasion of privacy.

Not answering him directly she said, "I think I am 4 months pregnant," and then began to cry.

"I think this is a great event for us. A first. This child will be an expression of the love between us. We are going to be great parents."

With that he could think of nothing else to say. He held her in his arms and the three of them rocked together.

Willie was born a month early. He required special care because his lungs were not fully developed. Gaul had a nursery set up in their quarters. From the moment of his birth, life dramatically changed. Willie's needs came first. For the first year he had a terrible habit of getting up in the night and screaming. It was not a normal night feeding. For a little fellow he would give out a blood curdling scream and wait for Mom to come and pick him up. Once he knew she was up, he would fall asleep. It drove Jocelyn crazy because she could never get a full night's sleep. For his part Gaul simply was so tired from the day's duties that he just slept through it all. It was a constant source of friction.

Gaul had become a student of history. He believed that the current generation with the exception of a few was not salvageable. It would always be a generation who accepted good order without question, and remain suspicious and unreceptive to democratic institutions. Change had to be brought about in a radical manner. He thought to himself, how do you change the demeanor of an entire society?

Gaul buzzed his adjutant. "Get Garrett Winslow and have him here in the next 30 minutes!"

A bedraggled Garrett Winslow appeared at reception 20 minutes later. He was accompanied by two Military Police Officers of the Legion. They did not hold him physically but their presence on either side of him was sufficient to gain his compliance.

He entered Gaul's office.

"Garrett, good of you to come. I'm glad to see that you made it through the troubles unharmed."

The fear in Garrett's eyes abated. If Gaul had intended to do him harm he would not be treating him like this.

"I've been studying what you did and what you knew when you worked for Secretary Warden. In fact I am quite familiar with it. What puzzles me is that you did nothing to expose what you knew."

Garrett wondered which way Gaul was going with this information. Was he being set up for a fall or was there something else?

"I see you as a very smart man, a weak man but someone who can emerge from the shadows and do something that is very good for the country."

Garrett started to protest, but Gaul put up his hand and said, "No! Hear me out!"

"I didn't start this revolution because I wanted to be the next Secretary. Power is not the commodity I value. It actually started quite by accident. I was like you in many respects. I was not an academic with a specialized field, but was the best of my kind in the organized killing of men who were perceived as enemies of the State. Quite by accident I came across the Library. I began to read. The more I read, the more I realized the moral shortcoming of our present state. We were living in a very dark age where the uniqueness of the individual ceased to be recognized. We treated people as cogs, and called them units. They were like fungible grains of sand in a hour glass. I became a revolutionary. I don't want our revolution to simply replace an earlier form of despotic government. At the same time I know the adult generation is lost. If this country is to be restored to its greatness then it has to be done through our children."

Garrett sat in stony silence not knowing what to say or do. He perceived that he was the full focus of Gaul's attention.

"What would you have me do?"

"That's what I wanted to hear. I am going to give you the broad outline of what I want, and will leave it to you to implement policy. I expect you to access the Library and create a curriculum for the education of children. You can pick anyone you want to assist you. I've given orders that your instructions are the same as a direct order from me. We have to save the children. They are our hope. In time this adult generation will die off. I want to see the emergence of a new kind of American who is filled with hope and respect for his fellow human beings."

Garrett swallowed hard. His would have a place in history books. He had no interest in any close relationship with another person. This opportunity was made to order. He would be the great scholar. His memory would be venerated through all time. Recognizing that he was merely imagining his own place in history, he thanked Gaul and left without further comment. Now he had to implement the idea.

Chapter 34

Maribeth Cooper 2

Maribeth kept asking herself, "What would be different now that the revolution had taken place?" She wondered how her life would change. Would it be for the better or would the same old habits of the repressive Secretariat return? She could not reconcile her thoughts. The new leadership promised so much, but she had seen so much that was wrong with the old leadership. How can you trust the government?

By now news of the Library was a public matter. Only the top scholars and academicians were allowed access to the Library. Somehow that chapped her the wrong way. It did not seem fair to her that in the old United States there was almost universal access to information. Of course she amused herself when she thought about this idea because even in old America government secrets were only accessible under the Freedom of Information Act. The Act was a tenuous way of holding the politicians accountable. She longed for access to the Library. She was now a woman of 35 and knew her mind. Sitting at her desk she penned a letter to General Gaul.

Dear General Gaul,

As the Supreme leader of the United States, I have a request to make. I hope you will look favorably on my request. I am a cataloguer of Government Documents. I have read all of the documents I assigned to our repository. All of my life I've asked the question of why things are as they exist. My great hope in life is to explore the Library so that I can answer the question, "Why?"

Respectfully,

Maribeth Cooper

For days she sat and stared at her note. She was frightened to send it because it would draw attention to her. Conversely there was a burning inside of her that said, "I want to know." In the end she hit the button on her computer that sent the note to General Gaul. She really did not expect any kind of answer, after all he was inundated with constant communication and demand for his time. At least she had tried. She felt better for it.

Chapter 35

The Trial 2

Dean Evan had become more than a mere Dean. He considered it his sacred mission in life to establish the judiciary as an independent branch of the government that was accountable to no one. He took to calling himself the Chief Justice. With his group of 20 he immersed himself in the Constitutional and criminal law of the United States as it existed from the inception of the Court to the Great War.

He considered his appointment as Dean to be tantamount to his appointment as Chief Justice. There may have been a slight of hand trick involved, but he believed it was of little consequence in these troubled times. Gaul as the titular head of government had the power to appoint a judiciary and had done so. What he lacked in legal scholarship he made up for in announcing an independent judiciary that was a co-existing branch of government, that was equal in all respect to the executive branch of government.

The country still lacked a legislature, but bright young men and women were rising up and voicing their opinions to create a collective consciousness that would serve as the legislative branch of government. The country was in transition, and anything could happen.

The first act of the Chief Justice was to assemble a tribunal for the trial of Secretary Warden, Gunter Ras and their cronies. There had not been a real trial for 3,000 years.

What had passed for a trial in the last 30 centuries, was a confession of guilt and a plea for mercy. Mercy was an arbitrary and capricious devil that lacked uniform administration and application. This practice had to stop.

Chief Justice Evan announced the formation of a tribunal, a courtroom where the case against the defendants would be made or lost based on a level playing field and the rules of evidence. Evidence was a difficult concept because in the years since the Great War the refined rules of admissibility had been altered and were unrecognizable.

Evan called an assemblage of the new advocates. He announced that the indictment and trial of the defendants would take place in one year. He believed it would take that long to assemble the evidence and marshal the defenses of the defendants.

There would be no rush to judgment. It was important to clearly demonstrate the excesses and abuses of the past; and if the defendants were found complicit beyond a reasonable doubt the punishment must be severe so as to set a standard for future conduct. History was being made.

Evan was not without his critics. That is the interesting thing about democracy. Give a man the right to speak his mind and he instantly becomes a political pundit. These times were no different.

Evan took a page from history. He had read the case of Marbury v. Madison that was so deeply ingrained in the federal collective consciousness. He simply announced, "The law is what the Court says it is." The Court had once again assumed the power of judicial review.

The trial of the defendants was to take place in the Great Hall of the People and was open to 1,000 spectators. In addition, cameras would record every word that was said and a simultaneous nationwide broadcast would be made to every home in the country.

The first two defendants to be tried were Chairman Warden and Gunter Ras. They were led into the courtroom with heavy security. Each waived to the assembled crowd and there was some cheering for them in the gallery. They smiled as if they were going on a Sunday picnic in the park. They were oblivious to the proceedings that were about to take place.

"I'll not tolerate any outbursts in the gallery." Evan said. "I expect everyone to be quiet, restrain themselves and not interfere in the proceedings. Anyone who violates this order will be summarily removed and not allowed to return on another day!"

With that the defendants took their seats in the defendants' doc. They were separated from their attorneys by a few feet. Each defendant was assigned two lead attorneys, and each attorney had a cadre of clerks and secretaries for support staff.

Defense counsel for the accused had been chosen for their intelligence, wit and ability to examine all sides of an issue. They did not particularly like their clients, but recognized that much more was at stake than their client's fate. True their clients might hang, but what was more important was to prove there was an equal system of justice and fair play for all people, no matter how enormous or brutal the crime.

Danny Dannenberg was the lead attorney for Gunter Ras. Dannenberg was a stickler for detail. He could be counted on to examine every factual aspect of the prosecution's case looking for the slightest flaw in order to break the glass. He was smart, ambitious and determined to make his mark.

Tom Mullins was lead counsel for Chairman Warden. In another life Mullins would have made a great bartender. He was toothy, friendly and dangerous. He could listen to a story like a good bartender or sell a story like he was a used car salesman.

Mullins and Dannenberg were pitted against a lone prosecutor, Josh Davis. In another life Josh Davis would have been a movie star cowboy. He was tall, lanky and soft spoken. All of his friends found him slow to anger. He had a keen wit and was known to drink too much and chase too many women. Still, the measure of a man is the level of his professional performance, not the dirt of his social life.

A year before the actual commencement of the trial, the Chief Justice explained to all of the players that there must be a fair trial.

"I don't want to try this case for the next 50 years. Take your best shot at each of the defendants. If you don't have the evidence they will walk free. I expect you to share what you have with each other, subject to the right of the defense to shield its work product from the prosecution. I say that because the state always has more power than the individual and I am going to keep the playing field level. I don't want to know anything about your case or the evidence you will produce until the time of trial. If anyone tries to back door me, he is going to be in serious trouble."

Mullins and Dannenberg furiously met with their clients before trial. They met separately and jointly, and explained the defenses available. The problem with the case was that Chairman Warden was charged with sedition and as the overseer of mass murder, while Gunter Ras was merely charged with a single count of murder. In a kinder time, their cases would have been severed and each would have received a separate trial.

Mullins filed a pretrial motion for severance.

"Your honor, the crimes that are charged against these two people bear no factual resemblance to each other. It is to the great prejudice of my client, Chairman Warden that she be tried in the same doc with a common murderer."

"What do you say Mr. Dannenberg?"

"Well sir, I think the same issue applies to my client. My client is simply indicted for a single count of murder. Chairman Warden is accused of killing thousands. There is no comparison in culpability. Her egregious conduct will rub off on my client to his disadvantage. It is simply not fair."

"Counsel, the Court has considered your objections to a joint trial. If this were a trial by jury the Court could understand the potential prejudice that would inure to the disadvantage of each party. Since this is a trial by the Bench, I believe this Court can sufficiently factually segregate the alleged crimes. Motion denied."

Chapter 36

Trial Testimony

The Court: "The clerk will read the indictment against the accused."

By the Clerk:

"The indictment against Chairman Warden charges as follows:

Count 1: On or about February 1, 5031, Defendant Chairman Warden did engage in the crime of Mass Murder by intentionally and indiscriminately authorizing the killing of 552 children between the ages of 4 and 7 years old at the Bionics East Facility in Buffalo, Kansas.

Count 2. On or about January 1, 5025 and continuing through May 1, 5030, Defendant Chairman Warden did willfully and unlawfully commit the crime of treason by disloyalty to the sovereign law of the United States of America in that she betrayed the sacred trust of her position and subverted the good of the country to her quest for personal autocratic power.

Count 3. On or about April 25, 5030, Defendant Chairman Warden did willfully and unlawfully conspire with Gunter Ras and others to murder Leslie Marcus, and in furtherance of the conspiracy Leslie Marcus met her death at the hands of Gunter Ras.

Count 4. On or about January 1, 2025 and continuing through May 1, 5030, Defendant Chairman Warden did willfully and unlawfully commit the crime of sedition by advocating and participating in acts against the lawful authority of the United States of America."

The Court: "How do you plead, guilty or not guilty?"

Before her attorneys could enter a plea, Chairman Warden jumped up from her chair.

"I do not recognize the authority or legitimacy of this Court. This Court has no jurisdiction over me. You're simply making up the rules as you go. You cannot try me because you are not the legitimate government of the United States. I refuse to participate in this mockery of justice."

With that she sat down. The Chief Justice looked over to Tom Mullins.

The Court: "Counsel what do you have to say about your client's statement?"

Mullins appeared nonpulsed by the statement.

Mullins: "Your honor, I believe the Chairman has a legitimate point. How can this Court assume to try her for crimes that were committed before the existence of this Court as a judicial body? This is a fundamental issue this Court is going to have to overcome. I believe she has a valid point. In this case the victor of the revolution is making up the new rules. These rules did not previously exist. It is fundamentally unfair to try her under this set of rules."

The Chief Justice had done his job well. Here it was the first day of trial when he believed all should have been going smoothly, and Advocate Mullins was challenging the jurisdiction of this Court to even entertain the case. The judiciary was alive and well, but from a public policy standpoint he could not allow this challenge to be sustained.

The Court: "Counsel the Court will take the objections of Chairman Warden under submission. In the meantime the Clerk will read the indictment against Gunter Ras."

The Clerk: "Gunter Ras, the indictment reads as follows:

Count 1. On or about April 25, 5030, Gunter Ras and Chairman Warden did willfully and unlawful conspire with others to murder

Leslie Marcus, and in furtherance of the conspiracy Leslie Marcus met her death at the hands of Gunter Ras."

The Court: "How do you plead, guilty or not guilty?"

Gunter Ras: "Not guilty, I was only following orders. I was a soldier and was taught that unquestioned obedience was the rule of law. Whatever I did was in my capacity as a soldier; I was only following orders."

The Court: "The Court will enter a not guilty plea on behalf of the defendant."

The Chief Justice then turned his attention to Josh Davis. "Mr. Davis do you have any opening statement to make to the Court?"

Josh Davis had one abiding quality. He reeked of integrity. He would have made a good advocate for the prosecution or the defense. His principal short coming was that he tended to view the world and the law in broad brush strokes. He did not always pay attention to details. This was his first trial. The eyes of the nation were clearly focused on him. It was better to display moral integrity at the expense of case detail.

Josh proceeded to address the Court.

Mr. Davis: "Your honor, the United States is going to prove all of the charges in the indictment to be true beyond a reasonable doubt."

He then proceeded to provide the Court with a roadmap of where he was going with his evidence. Tom Mullins could not contain himself as Josh was addressing the Court in his opening statement. He jumped up from his seat.

Tom Mullins: "Your Honor with all due respect to my esteemed colleague, on behalf of Chairman Warden, I have filed a motion in liminie to preclude any testimony being offered with respect to the charges of treason and sedition as contained in the indictment. The basis of the motion in liminie is that this judicial body did not exist as a court of law at the time the alleged offenses occurred. In point of fact there was no judicial body in existence to try the issues presented in

Count 1 and 2 of the indictment. As such the charges were made after the fact and constitute an ex post facto law. It is fundamental that in any court of law an accused cannot be charged for a offense that was not a crime at the time it was committed. It is even more egregious in this case because this very government and its court system did not exist at the time of the alleged offense. On behalf of the Chairman, I respectfully request an immediate ruling on this matter because if evidence is allowed to come in on this issue it will cloud the other issues before the Court to the disadvantage of my client."

Mullins stood at the lectern. He had made his case. He had set the predicate that questioned the very jurisdiction of this Court to proceed with the trial.

The Chief Justice was faced with two conflicting directions. As a matter of public policy and for the preservation of the revolution it was necessary to try the previous government for its crimes against the people of the United States. Conversely, it must not appear that the victor in the revolution was making the rules as matters went along after the fact. The system had to appear to be fair, regardless of outcome. This was not a trial where the accused pleaded guilty and requested mercy from the Court.

The Chief Justice was reminded of a line he had read in one of the old cases.

"Hard cases make bad law!"

The Court: "The Court is going to take a short recess to consider Mr. Mullins' motion. The Court will see counsel in chambers."

In Chambers:

Mr. Mullins: "Your honor, I want a reporter in here so that everything is on the record. I don't want any ambiguities about what I said or what the Court said with respect to my motion."

The Chief Justice was amused. Mullins not only had read the old cases, he was a total adversary committed to his client. He could suddenly see how messy trials could be, and how uncertain their outcome depending on the advocacy and skill of the advocates involved.

The Court: "Counsel, I am going to give you 24 hours to provide further points and authorities in support of your motion on behalf of Defendant Warden. The Court has not made a decision in this matter on how it is going to proceed. The Court is not satisfied with the claims and authorities cited in behalf of the motion. There is more here at stake than the charges against the defendants. The Court expects you to go back to the books and sort it out. I will expect your brief no later than 24 hours from now."

Two days following, proceedings were resumed. There was a hushed silence in the courtroom. Everyone sat in anticipation of what the ruling of the Court would be. Amongst the more enlightened there was a fear that the charges against the Chairman would be dismissed, and if this happened she would lead a further counter revolution against the United States. Few saw this matter as the exercise of the prerogative of an independent judiciary. After all there had been no experience with democratic institutions for over 3,000 years.

Like everyone else in the Citadel, Gaul sat glued to his monitor watching the trial unfold.

The monitor covered a 200 inch panel on his wall. He could see shots from every direction of the participants and spectators in the courtroom.

The trial was making history. It was to be the first fair trial in 3,000 years. Gaul found himself amused at Dean Evan. He now referred to himself as the Chief Justice and took to wearing a black robe with five white chevrons on each sleeve. He made an imposing appearance. His dark black hair now had rivers of silver running through it. His face appeared gaunt and deeply lined. Anyone seeing him for the first time was instantly struck by his stark appearance.

The Chief Justice sat on a raised dais. The bench itself was carved out of hardwood from what was once Louisiana. To his right sat the Clerk with his row of assistants. Spaced throughout the courtroom were marshals hired by the Chief Justice, whose function was to keep the peace, maintain good order the protect the Court. Seated five feet below the Chief Justice and separated by 25 feet were the attorneys for the United States and the defense. The defendants were to the right of their counsel. There was no jury. Juries would not return until the present generation was reduced to headstones in a nameless graveyard.

The Chief Justice had just dismissed Counts 2 and 4 of the indictment against the Chairman. The courtroom was in an uproar. Spectators were shouting that the trial was rigged and there was no justice, this was just another good-old-boys court.

The situation was getting out of hand and the Court ordered the marshals to clear the courtroom. A recess was declared until 10 a.m. on the day following.

Gaul was incensed when he saw what had taken place. He kept thinking to himself that the CJ had sabotaged the revolution. He saw a crisis of confidence undercutting all the work he had done. He kept repeating to himself, "How can he do this, what the hell is wrong with him?"

He yelled out to his adjutant, "Get the CJ on the horn now!"

A few minutes later his adjutant returned.

"Sir, I am sorry but he says he cannot talk to you, that he is in the middle of the case."

"You tell that son of bitch to get on the horn or I am going to send a hundred Legionaries over and bring him and his whole damn courtroom over here."

"Yes Sir."

A few moments later there was a call from the CJ.

"Gaul I don't understand what your problem is. I'm in the middle of the most important trial in the last 3,000 years and you're interfering."

Gaul began to turn a bright red but contained himself.

"My problem is that you're about to let that bitch off. That cannot happen! She has to be found guilty and executed in the most public way possible so that her kind of government never comes back."

There was silence on the phone. Finally in a measured tone of voice Gaul heard the following words:

"Gaul, you created an independent judiciary. You wanted courts that upheld the rule of law. You did not want the results to be predetermined. Every case was to rise or fall on the evidence, not some public policy you were seeking to enforce. You got what you wanted. An independent judiciary. The rule of law. Now you do not like it because you are uncertain what the result is going to be. That's democracy my friend. That's how courts work in a real democracy. You cannot preordain the conclusion. If you do the revolution has no purpose. Personally I think that Josh Davis got a little over zealous when he charged Warden with sedition and treason. The evidence was not there. I've read lots of old cases where over zealous prosecutors over charged and got their noses bloodied. That's what happens. There are other charges and if the evidence is there they will stick. You can't forget we are building a new system of responsible government. That is what you and I believe in."

Gaul was speechless. It was true what the CJ was saying. But he was also risking everything they had fought for in the revolution. Was this how democracy worked? It was one fragile system. The CJ had already made his ruling. It was too later to turn around. The Gordian knot had been cut. Gaul realized there was a vast difference between what was written in the history books and the actual practice of democracy.

The CJ had one final word.

"By the way Gaul, don't tell me what the sentence will be if she's found guilty. Sentencing is purely within the discretion of the court on a case by case basis!"

With that the CJ hung up.

Gaul wondered what kind of monster he had unleashed.

The Court: "Mr. Davis, call your first witness."

Josh Davis: "The United States calls medical officer, Major Jonathan Marsh."

The Clerk: "State your first and last name."

Witness: "Jonathan Marsh."

The Clerk: "Do you affirm that you will tell the whole truth and give your best recollection to this Honorable Court?"

Witness: "I do."

Josh Davis: "State your business or occupation."

Witness: "Medical Officer, Major, assigned to the Kinder Haus at Buffalo, Kansas."

Josh Davis: "How long did you work at that facility?"

Witness: "Approximately 10 years."

Josh Davis: "What were the inclusive dates of your assignment?"

Witness: "January 1, 5021 to December 31, 5030."

Josh Davis: "Do you have any special training or knowledge that qualifies you as a medical officer?"

Witness: "Yes sir, I graduated from medical school and did a residence in gene splicing and genetics. Thereafter, I continued my education and obtained a PhD in advanced genetic engineering from the University of Illinois. I then returned to active duty with the Legion and was assigned to supervise genetic harvesting and outplacement separations at the Kinder Haus in Buffalo, Kansas."

Tom Mullins: "Your honor may I have the witness on voir dire? There are some important foundational issues that need to be explored if we are going to continue."

The Court: "That's quite irregular so early in the proceeding. Approach the bench and we'll have a sidebar conference."

Davis, Mullins and Dannenberg approached the bench. There was a hushed air of silence in the courtroom because no one knew what to anticipate.

"What's this all about counsel?"

Mullins looked to Dannenberg and deferred to him.

"Your honor, I believe Mr. Dannenberg can best explain this situation."

Dannenberg was a bit hesitant to jump into the fray because the offer of proof he was about to make may have been tainted by illegally securing the evidence. On the other hand the United States had not disclosed this piece of exculpatory evidence to the defense, and it was better to put it in the face of the court and prosecutor so that a fair trial was ensured.

"Well sir, it's come to my attention that Major Marsh has been offered an incentive for his testimony. Actually it's a rather large incentive. He's made a deal with the prosecution that in exchange for his testimony he will not be prosecuted for complicity in the mass murder of the children that were at the Kinder Haus. To my way of thinking that taints his testimony. I don't think he can be fair and objective and I'm moving to strike all of his prospective testimony."

The CJ did a slow burn. Suddenly Josh Davis knew he was in trouble. Like many other inexperienced prosecutors he thought he could float the evidence without disclosing the behind the scene deal he had made with the witness. He knew he was skating on thin ice and that depending on the mood of the CJ he might find himself standing in the defendant's dock for his unseemly conduct.

"Mr. Davis, when did you intend to inform the defense of this so-called deal?"

"Well your Honor, I really did not think it was relevant because the Major was just going to testify as to what he saw and heard. It's all above board."

The explanation did not fly with the CJ.

The Court: "Permission to take the witness on voir dire is granted."

Dannenberg: "Major Marsh is it true that you have been granted full immunity from prosecution for any crimes committed at the Kinder Haus in exchange for your testimony in this matter?"

Witness: "I was told I would never be asked this question."

The Court: "Answer the question."

Witness: "Yes, that is what I was promised."

Dannenberg: "Were you promised anything else?"

Witness: "Just that nothing would happen to my wife and we'd be able to go on and live our lives in a normal manner."

Dannenberg: "Your honor, I submit that the testimony of this witness is so tainted by his motive to survive, that it is not trustworthy and cannot be used as an evidentiary basis against either defendant in this proceeding."

The Court: "What does the United States have to say in this matter?"

Davis: "Your honor, before the revolution we were living in a police state.

Everything done in the name of the state was secretive and hidden behind memos marked "Classified" or "Top Secret." There were secret organizations within the parameters of government that precluded the people from knowing what was going on or taking place in the name of the people. The only means available to remove this black curtain is by turning over known or suspected wrongdoers and giving them grants of immunity in exchange for their testimony. That's exactly what has occurred in this case. We balanced the equities involved and came to the conclusion that our cause was just and that we should proceed."

From his distant vantage point Gaul choked on his beer. Another major screw up by the CJ. This case was being mishandled from the very top.

The CJ swiveled in his chair. His back was now to the attorneys and crowded courtroom. Even he did not anticipate such conduct. Bad parts of the old judicial system were coming back. He feared matters would not right themselves. He was appalled that the United States Attorney could not distinguish his conduct from that of the predecessor regime. On the other hand it was best to let the evidence come out. The weight of the witness' testimony could always be challenged by other admissible evidence.

Josh Davis: "Major Marsh, how many children were at the Kinder Haus in 5030?"

The witness: "I don't have an exact count, approximately 600 to the best of my recollection."

Josh Davis: "With regard to the 600 children what was your responsibility or function?"

Major Marsh hesitated. Here he was before so many cameras. Everything he said was being recorded. For a moment he reflected on his role in the nasty business of selection.

The witness: "My function was to select those units who were fit to go on for further education, possibly for the Legion and to designate those who had the mental and physical prowess to do well in our society."

Josh Davis: "And the other's; what was to become of them?"

The witness: "They were selected, of course."

Josh Davis: "What does that mean, they were selected?"

Major Marsh looked very uncomfortable in the witness dock. The nose of his weasel-like face began to noticeably twitch as he rocked himself from side to side.

The witness: "Well these were just units. Units you know. We salvaged body parts where they were needed, and we disposed of the rest of the units."

Josh Davis: "Major Marsh, you keep referring to these children as units. Weren't they in fact just children? Wouldn't it be better to call them children?"

Mr. Mullin: "Objection your honor, counsel is badgering the witness. He can only answer one question at a time."

The Court: "Objection overruled. The Court believes Major Marsh understood the question. Just to be certain, did you understand the question or did you not Major?"

The witness: "Yes sir, I did."

Josh Davis: "Answer the question Major!"

The witness: "I suppose you could call them children. They were just bred. What do you want me to say? Yes, they were children, but they were defective."

Josh Davis: "When you say they were just bred, are you saying that the Central Bionics Lab and the Kinder Haus bore no responsibility for their safety and well being?"

The witness: "Yes, of course, they were just defective units!"

Josh Davis: "By whose standards were they defective units?"

The witness: "By the standards of the Secretariat."

Josh Davis: "Did you have some orders from the Secretariat on what you were to do with the defective units?"

The witness: "Yes, I had an order personally signed by Secretary Warden that the defective units were to be farmed for body parts and disposed of."

Josh Davis: "Do you have that order with you today?"

Major Marsh reached into his grey tunic. He pulled out an order that was signed by Secretary Warden that confirmed his instructions.

Josh Davis: "I am showing the order to Counsel. I have previously furnished defense counsel with a copy of the Order. I ask that it be marked for identification subject to it being authenticated by an appropriate handwriting expert's testimony in this proceeding."

The Court: "It will be marked as Exhibit 1."

Josh Davis: "How did you dispose of the defective units?"

Suddenly Major Marsh's face was filled with color. His heart began to beat at an accelerated rate. He knew the final latch was being set.

The witness: "Each unit was given a shot in the jugular vein that instantly rendered it unconscious. Clinical death followed within 3 minutes. It was all quite painless and medically sound."

Josh Davis: "You mean each child was murdered with a shot of poison?"

The witness: "Well I supposed you could put it that way, but they were just defective units."

Josh Davis: "And the bodies, Doctor, what did you do with the bodies?"

The witness: "Well we couldn't have them taking up too much space so we just disposed of them."

Josh Davis: "How did you dispose of them?"

The witness: "We burned them and reduced them to unrecognizable ash."

Josh Davis: "How many children were murdered in 5030?"

Tom Mullins: "Objection, the state has failed to establish that anyone was murdered let alone a large number of children. There are no bodies; there is no evidence of the crime to corroborate the testimony of the witness."

The Court: "Overruled, we don't need the presence of a dead body to prove that a homicide occurred."

Josh Davis: "Again Major, how many children were murdered at Buffalo, Kansas in 5030?"

The witness: "400, 500 maybe 600. I can't give you an exact number."

Josh Davis: "Were there any other Kinder Hauses besides the one at Buffalo, Kansas?"

The witness: "Yes."

Josh Davis: "How many?"

The witness: "Spread throughout the country I know of at least 50."

Josh Davis: "Were the practices at the other Kinder Haus any different than at your facility?"

The witness: "No of course not, everything was quite uniform. The standards were the same."

When it came time to cross-examine Major Marsh it was clear to the defense that they had to tread very lightly on his testimony. To deny the events he recited would be to deny their own history. Conversely it was important to place the events in context so that the activities of Superintendent Warden could be appreciated for the value that she brought to the community. The defense of necessity had never been used in this context where so much life had been violated. Conversely, the many witnesses that were paraded in front of the Court and cameras made it impossible to dispute the facts of the indictment.

There is an old expression that dead men tell no tales. For the most part that is true. Gunter Ras had carefully covered his tracks in the death of Leslie Marcus. All of the Legionnaires who could have testified against him were dead. He felt confident that he would be found not guilty and he would be returned to his post in the Legion.

Josh Davis fretted that Gunter Ras would go free. He thought of him as the lowest piece of scum in the ocean. Such men did not deserve to live. In spite of all of this he had not been able to marshal strong evidence against Ras. There were no percipient witnesses left. As he concluded his case against Secretary Warden he knew the moment of truth was coming as to Gunter Ras. He would either have to dismiss the case or look like the biggest fool before the entire country. Neither solution was acceptable to him. He kept pushing his investigators to take another look at the case and to find physical evidence that would help him. He was running out of time.

A break came in the case 35 minutes before he was due back in the courtroom. His chief investigator came running into his office in a breathless manner.

"Josh, I think we have something. In fact I know we do. I just need a few hours to rewire the camera of one of the security people that participated in the death of Leslie Marcus."

Josh was astounded by the idea that they had something.

"Do we really have something solid or is this just another dead end? I need to know your best shot! Tell me what we've got. I can't go back in that courtroom and make a complete idiot of myself."

"Josh, I think we've got it but I need a few hours."

"OK, I'm going to get you a few hours, but that's it."

Josh had quickly learned the tricks of the trial trade. When he walked back into the courtroom he appeared to be sweating profusely and was unstable on his feet. His apparent physical problem was obvious to all.

The Court: "Mr. Davis are you ill?"

Josh Davis: "No sir, I will try to proceed."

The Court: "Mr. Bailiff, bring that man up here."

Josh found himself slung over the shoulder of a 6'6, 285 pound bailiff who lifted him as though he was a feather.

The CJ put his hand on Josh's forehead and felt the hot sweat trickling from his pores.

The Court: "This man is ill. The trial cannot continue under these conditions.

The Court is declaring a 24 hour recess."

Josh's investigator got his time. He took the camera to the forensic science lab where two electronics experts hovered over it.

"Can you recover its memory?"

"We'll try."

The technicians were not able to recover all of the camera's memory, but partially succeeded.

The Court: "Call your next witness Mr. Davis."

Josh Davis: "The United States calls electronics technician Roselyn Miles."

Josh Davis meticulously established her credentials, the chain of evidence on how she came into possession of the camera and her salvaging of part of the memory contained in the camera. The moment of truth was at hand. He would ask her to play what the camera recorded in its memory. Josh Davis: "Ms. Miles, would you please play for the benefit of the Court that portion of the record you were able to recover from the memory of the dead

Legionnaire's camera."

The witness: "Yes."

The sound track of the camera recorded the words of Gunter Ras.

"Leslie, do you want to talk? Now is the time. It is now or never!"

"Gunter, I am only 25, I've not lived yet. Please let me live. Please do not kill me."

It showed Gunter turning to his henchman and lifting his finger to his face. That was all it contained.

All eyes in the courtroom turned to Gunter. His face was flushed. He started to cough in nervous fashion.

The evidence continued to mount against the defendants. Their defense counsel interposed every technical objection possible to the admissibility of the evidence. Sometimes there is nothing a lawyer can do, but to be certain that his client has received due process. This was turning out to be one of those cases; however the defense still had two powerful theories to advance on behalf of their clients.

Tom Mullins: "Your honor, permission to address the Court."

The Court: "Go ahead sir."

Tom Mullins: "Your honor on behalf of both of our clients I am moving for a directed verdict of acquittal. The crime of murder and mass murder did not exist under the law of the Secretariat. It was made a crimes after the revolution, and our clients cannot be tried or held accountable for matters which were not crimes under the prior government law. It is as plain as the nose on your face that these matters were not crimes under the law of the Secretariat and to now make these people accountable is not only manifestly unfair but denies them due process in every respect. The cases should be dismissed and our clients should be left to go on their way and continue with their lives."

The Chief Justice looked at defense counsel in disbelief. It was inconceivable to him that this manner of argument could be advanced to save the necks of these two criminals. At the same time he knew that he must deliver a soundly reasoned and impassioned response.

The Court: "Counsel in anticipation of the possibility that you might raise this claim as a defense the Court on its own has undertaken substantial research into the cultural history of human institutions dating back to the first recorded history. In all of our human history murder has never been sanctioned in any culture. The concept of state sponsored mass murder such as took place in Buffalo, Kansas is not acceptable in any culture. Intentional and indiscriminate killing by government agents, whether they have a badge or piece of paper setting forth their authority, is morally wrong, reprehensible and punishable regardless of whether there is a law of government that prohibits such conduct. It is simply unacceptable. Your motion for a directed verdict is denied. You may make your opening statement or call your first witness."

Trials are not always cracked up to what they are supposed to be. Usually one side or the other has the dominant evidence. In criminal cases such as murder and mass murder the standard of proof was guilt beyond a reasonable doubt. Not all doubt but simply put, when weighing the evidence the prosecution had the burden of establishing the criminal culpability of the defendant, and the defense had not created a reasonable doubt with respect to the culpability of the defendant.

The case against Secretary Warden and Gunter Ras might well have played out in a 21st Century courtroom in front of a jury. Unfortunately for each of them there was little wiggle room. Each in his own way was like the murder suspect caught with the smoking gun in hand and the dead body at their feet. Secretary Warden could feel the noose tightening around her neck.

Mullins and Dannenberg consoled each other with the thoughts that their obligations as defense counsel was not to have their clients found factually innocent, but that they were there to insure their clients had a fair trial, due process and were given every opportunity to defend themselves. In the end it was the old public defender game. Neither Mullins nor Dannenberg had fire in their belly for the defense of their clients. Their fire was to extol a new system of justice that afforded equal rights and equal access to judicial resources for all people. What they railed against was arbitrary oppression without standards or appellate review.

In the course of preparing for trial they knew in their heart of hearts that the defense of their clients was probably hopeless because of the overwhelming evidence against them. Their collective respect for the Chief Justice and the institution he was fostering was immense because he had proven in one fell swoop that justice would not be denied because of political expediency. Beyond that they could not hope to accomplish more.

Each of them had studied the trial transcripts of old criminal cases in the archives of the Library. Little insight was to be had from the old dusty records. If anything, each reached the conclusion when you have nothing to work with for the defense, pound the table or try the prosecutor. It was inconceivable that such a dog and pony show would fly in this case. If there were to be a defense in this case and if there ever is a defense to murder it must be based upon a truthful set of values that does not offend one's humanity. It seemed to Mullins that these were irreconcilable objectives.

Mullins entered the attorney client section of the Citadel Jail. He heard the metal door clang behind him. In a few minutes Secretary Warden entered the small room. The room was painted battleship grey. They were physically separated by a small conference table. Their view of the world was a universe apart.

"Madam Secretary, we have to put on a defense. I don't have a factual defense and you have not provided me with any. If we don't do something the Chief Justice is going to find you guilty and you will hang as a common criminal. What do you want me to do?"

Secretary Warden looked at Mullins. He was a nice young man. A bit naive in the affairs of state, but certainly capable as any of defending her in this matter.

"I have done nothing wrong. I acted to preserve and protect the Secretariat and everything that it stands for."

"With all due respect Madam Secretary, the United States has proven that you are responsible for the deaths of thousands of children. We have to counter those facts."

"Young man, I am not responsible for the deaths of any children. They were simply units that were defective. Where possible, organs and body parts were salvaged for the good of the rest of the population. There is no reason to feed and house these units. They will never be useful to society. I had a duty to do the greatest good for the greatest number of people. I carried out my duty. The fact that some mentally and physically defective units were disposed of is of little concern to me. You have to look at the totality of the situation."

"But Madam Secretary, those units as you call them were children. They carried the same genes that you and I carry. The fact that they were mentally or physically slow was a luck of the draw in the gene splice. Don't you have any feelings at all for them? This judge is going to rip your guts out unless you show some remorse. These were kids that were euthanized. Don't you get it?"

Secretary Warden starred back at him with a blank face. It was obvious that she and Mullins were not on the same page. What she viewed as units, Mullins viewed as human beings. How do you communicate when your view of the core issue is not the same?

Mullins was not to be deterred.

"What about the murder of Leslie Marcus?"

Her response was to repeat the interrogatory. "What about it? Leslie Marcus was an unfortunate casualty of our war against the usurpers of the government. She is of no consequence. Her presence or absence in life is of no note. She was not about to contribute any great discovery to the fund of human knowledge. She was a twit. At most she was the squeeze of Jocelyn Jones and we had to know what she knew. When she refused to talk she signed her own death warrant. It's as simple as that."

In an adjacent cell Dannenberg was having his meeting with Gunter Ras. Gunter was unable to accept the fact that he was a prisoner charged with a capital crime. He still fancied himself a member of the Inner Circle entitled to all the perks and pleasures of his station in life. Being treated as a common criminal was foreign to his way of thinking.

Dannenberg found himself going through the same mental exercise that Mullins was engaging with in his conversation with the Secretary.

"Gunter, I have no factual defense for you! We can attack the technician who recovered the film clip of you involving the death of Leslie Marcus, but that is not going to save you from the gallows. That film strip could not be faked. The worst part of it is when you lifted your finger to your face to finish her off. I don't care what you did or what your motives are or were. What I care about is saving you from dropping through that hole on the gallows floor. Give me something to work with. Help me to help you. So far you have given me nothing. I have nothing but my skill as an advocate. The judge wants to hear some justification for your conduct. There has to be some reasonable explanation that can be given to explain your conduct."

Gunter starred back at him and said nothing.

Finally he croaked out, "I was only following the orders of Secretary Warden."

Dannenberg got up, turned around and exclaimed out loud, "What a fucked up defense. Who the hell is going to believe this crap?" He returned to his apartment and proceeded to finish off a 5th of sour mash.

Two days later the trial resumed. Mullins called Secretary Warden to testify. Before he would let her testify the Chief Justice carefully questioned her and advised her of her rights.

"Good morning Madam Secretary. I want to go over your rights with you so that you have a clear understanding of the law as it applies to this case. I understand that your attorney has already so advised you; however since this is a capital case I feel it incumbent on the part of the Court to readvise you."

"Do you understand that you do not have to testify in this proceeding and that no one can compel you to testify?" Warden mumbled, "Yes."

"Do you understand that if you do testify whatever you say can be considered against you, and the United States Attorney will have the right to challenge you and cross examine you?"

Warden was in no mood to be deterred and she quickly assented to each question from the Court in short order.

Tom Mullins proceeded with her defense.

"Secretary Warden, you've heard the charges levied against you in the indictment?"

The witness: "Yes, I have."

Tom Mullins: "Are you guilty or not guilty?"

The witness: "I am not guilty of any crime against the United States or its people. I do not recognize the jurisdiction of this Court to try me for crimes allegedly committed before the operative date of this Court's existence."

Tom Mullins: "Chairman Warden, are you guilty of mass murder in the case of the children euthanized in Kansas?"

The Witness: "Young man I told you before and I will tell this Court, I am not responsible for the deaths of any children. They were simply units that were defective. Where possible, organs and body parts were salvaged for the good of the rest of the population. There is no reason to feed and house these units. They will never be useful to society. I had a duty to do the greatest good for the greatest number of people. I carried out my duty. The fact that some mentally and physically defective units were disposed of is of little concern to me. You have to look at the totality of the situation."

Tom Mullins: "Is there anything else you would like to add?"

The Witness: "Nothing!"

The Court: "Cross-Examination Mr. Davis?"

Josh Davis quickly considered the testimony he had just heard. The Secretary had condemned herself. Her arrogance and lack of humanity were a testament to her guilt.

Josh Davis: "The United States waives its right to cross-examine the defendant."

The case against Gunter Ras was much simpler. He was just a thug. In another age one might describe him as a hit man, a hanger on who did without question the bidding of those more intelligent.

Dannenberg had nothing to offer him aside from a technical defense that did not mitigate against the horrendous nature of his crime. Participation in beating a helpless woman to death who did not even know why she was being beaten to death did not speak of a decent man. It was the kind of conduct that one thinks of as thuggish.

Gunter Ras would never be the poster boy for the Legion. If anything he was a man without a soul, a man without a country, a man who was so self-centered as to deny any good. His life had no redeeming social value and he stood for nothing except self-actualization. This was the life that Dannenberg sought to save.

How can one achieve the impossible when all the facts are exposed to the light of day? Gunter Ras made Dannenberg feel dirty. Shaking the man's hand and having to sit next to him at trial caused Dannenberg to loath him. Still he did everything within his power to save him. It was an incongruous task with no reward at the end. What redeeming social value is adhered to if you save such a villain at the end of the day? Dannenberg could think of none, yet he continued to try his best.

The Chief Justice advised Ras of his rights, just as he had advised the Secretary. Ras was eager to testify.

Dannenberg: "Officer Ras is there something you want to tell this Court?"

The witness: "Yes there is."

Dannenberg: "You are free to make any comments you wish, but remember I have advised you that some or all of what you say may count against you."

The witness: "I understand and do not care. I do not recognize the legitimacy of this Court. I am a member of the Inner Circle, an officer of the Legion and am loyal to the Secretariat. You cannot try me for the crime of murder because I was only following the legally constituted orders of the Secretariat. I did nothing wrong. Leslie Marcus was aligned with an enemy of the State. Jocelyn Jones had the seditious writing of Thomas Paine in her quarters. She sought to overthrow the duly constituted government. Leslie Marcus was her lover. It was necessary and proper to extract the names of her coconspirators in order to preserve the Secretariat. I have nothing further to say. Long live the Secretariat."

With that he sat down and was silent. A black cloud fell over the courtroom. The truth of the murder had not come to light.

The Court: "This Court will be in recess for the next two days. In two days hence I will expect counsel to submit their closing arguments. Court is adjourned."

Chapter 37

Terrorism

Coordinated terrorist attacks struck the Citadel and lesser cities across the nation. The attack on the Citadel was the worst violence the city had seen since the commencement of the revolt.

There was a high civilian death toll. Instead of an attack from the air the insurgents seemed to come out of the general population and after doing their murderous business merged back into the population.

Dozens of people were killed as they sat in cinemas and restaurants enjoying the relaxation of the day. It was Sunday, a traditional day of rest in America. Few if any thought about the serious problems of the day. This was a day devoted to relaxation and play far removed from the troubling times.

From the air black pools of smoke made their way skyward. One would have thought the city was on fire in multiple locations. It was on fire but not as the result of a natural disaster. The city burned from the explosions set off by the insurgents.

Bombs, be they dropped from the air or set off in a crowded restaurant or market place are indiscriminate killing devices. Their explosive charge and shrapnel does not distinguish between young and old or social class. The explosive is simply designed to kill and maim as many as possible and inflict terror into the populace.

What was particularly gruesome were the bombs detonated at refueling stations. Gasoline had been used for thousands of years as a fuel. It had always had the capacity to burn and cause great injury. Bombs were simultaneously set off at 25 refueling stations. The physical damage to the infrastructure was not great. The emotional toll it took of the general population was devastating. Fire is man's friend and his greatest fear.

When the trial of Secretary Warden and General Ras commenced there was a vast element that felt they were about to be disenfranchised. Their privileges would be gone and they would have to make their way in a kinder society. They had neither the skills nor education to wander for the next 75 years. It was untenable that they who had run this society for so long would become the disenfranchised minority.

Such thoughts ran counter to their ideology, training and experience. They gathered in secret cells and waited for a leader to emerge.

In every society there had always been malcontents and persons of self anointed importance. The 51st Century was no different. Heinz Anderson was an angry man. With the coming of the revolt he saw his career shattered. He was a captain in the Legion. In time with a little luck and a few good assignments he would make it to the general staff. All he needed was to be at the right place and kiss enough ass to make it to the top.

He didn't know what was at the top or what to expect but it was certainly better than being a mere captain. He was resolved to do whatever it took to make the grade.

On the eve of the revolt he was playing poker with a major and two other captains. He quickly became aware that a great battle was taking place but he and his unit were confined to their base. He felt like he was missing his war and that all opportunity for advancement was connected to this war. Little did he realize that on the morning after the revolt the entire world would change and his place in it would no longer be assured.

He woke with a great sense of anxiety and anticipation. When the Chairman's trial was televised he went into a complete mental meltdown. This was the end of life as he knew it. He met with other young officers.

"We have to do something to show that we are still alive!"

"What do you suggest Heinz? What can we do? I think we are just screwed and that fate has dealt us a bad blow. Just born at the wrong time."

"You're wrong, there's lots of things we can do. We can become a force to be reckoned with. No one can stop us."

"Oh, yeah, what's our goal; what is our agenda?"

"I'm not sure yet, we will have to have some political agenda but for the time being we have to make their life hell."

"Easy to say, hard to do!"

"Well what would you do?"

"I don't know."

Everyone listened intently to the exchange.

"I don't want to be the next one on trial for treason. I just want to live my life and enjoy my time."

"Well if that's all you want then you don't belong here!"

"What are you saying?"

"I'm saying that we have to start our own revolution. We'll invent an ideology but for the time being we can say we are acting to preserve the Secretariat."

That's how the counter revolution was begun. It emerged out of the grab for power of the junior officers. They developed little cells where each officer knew the men in his cell, but not the men in other cells. This way their identities could be protected if they were apprehended. To the average Legionnaire it made no difference. Their code was obedience.

The attack on the Citadel took place before the final arguments were made in the trial of the Chairman and Gunter Ras. The attack was designed to disrupt the judicial proceedings and feed fear into the minds of the populace and new government. Most of all it was designed to send a message to the fledgling judiciary. The message was clear. "Don't convict the Secretary and Ras of anything or you will be next."

The Chief Justice flew into a rage. Everything was at stake in this trial. He had a long vision of what America could be again. Now this attack on the Citadel threatened all.

He picked up his communicator and placed a call to Gaul.

Looking at him on his view screen, Gaul tried to keep an impassive appearance.

"What can I do for you?"

"You damn well better stop this insurrection! Find who is responsible, lock them up and we'll bring them to trial!"

The Chief Justice was beginning to sound like the attorney general instead of the measured man in the black robe. Gaul could feel the strain come across the communicator. He too felt it. Silently he wondered to himself, "Was this to be the bloody French Revolution revisited?"

I'll do what I can, but in the meantime I believe we need to move perimeter security further out for the trial. I can't let them blow you up and allow the Chairman and Ras to be martyrs."

"Yes, I think you're right but it mustn't appear that we are creating our own version of the police state. Do you understand?"

Gaul knew exactly what the CJ was saying. The problem was to implement security within the confines of government that guaranteed freedom of movement and association. How to do what reads so easy on paper?

Gaul ordered the perimeter of the courthouse security to be moved 500 meters. That distance would not stop everyone, but it would provide a chance of survival in the event a terrorist broke through. Any greater distance would involve closing the trial. It was a balancing act.

He also ordered an increase in screening. Terrorists could break through by setting off a bomb at screening, and then pouring through the slot, but it was a chance that would have to be taken. This democracy business was a tough go. It was messy. There were always problems. He felt he had aged 20 years since the revolt began. He simply longed for a deserted location with Jocelyn where they could cling to each other in the stillness of the night and shut the world out.

The closing arguments of the trial were an anticlimax to the testimony. Josh Davis went through a meticulous recitation of the multiple crimes of horrific murder that was perpetrated on the children at the Kinder Haus. Spectators in the Gallery winced at his recitation. It was as if someone was driving spikes into their living tissue.

It was hard not to cry. Then he came to the case of Leslie Marcus. A large cameo of Leslie filled half the courtroom. It was easy to acknowledge she was physically beautiful. The women in the gallery wished their appearance was as pleasing as Leslie. The men wondered what it would have been like to have such a woman.

Josh described the beating to her face. Then he repeated her last words, "Gunter, I am only 25, I've not lived yet. Please let me live. Please do not kill me."

"I have nothing more your Honor. Whatever I say cannot bring these lives back. The children are faceless. We'll never know who they were, but there is a face to Leslie Marcus. She did not deserve to die like this."

Tom Mullins rose from his chair and surveyed the Gallery. There were some hard looking faces out there. He had ceased to believe in his client. Inside his head he felt only contempt for her, but this was not an emotion he could display. He was her advocate, and advocate he must be.

The case was no longer about her. It was about upholding a system of justice that had long been forgotten and was now being restored. He would play his role. He held a pen in hand and starred at it in singular concentration. All eyes in the courtroom focused on him. He stood there for 5 minutes.

The Court: "Mr. Mullins do you have something to say?"

Tom Mullins: "Your honor, this case isn't about my client. It's really about a corrupt system of government. My client was just the titular head of this government. It could have been anyone. As fate had it she was the one. She grew up in a dark age. She was not taught that all life has some intrinsic value, yet she is being held accountable to a new standard that maintains all life has intrinsic value. She was taught to protect the State, and that it was the State that was the giver and taker of life. In a sense she is no more than a pawn in a game whose rules were determined thousands of years ago. If General Gaul had not discovered the Library we would not be here today. Life would go on as usual and the Secretary would remain the central source of government power. As it is, all is now upside down. Circumstance has dictated reality. She is no more guilty of the crime of murder than anyone else in this room. She was merely upholding the institution of the State. I do not deny for a moment that people died, that children died and that Leslie Marcus was robbed of her life. Those are facts cast in bronze. However I put it to the Court that even though those lives are gone the crime of murder was not committed. What was done was in the interest of the State to preserve the perception of the American way of life. Life as we knew it, life as it had been for thousands of years. This was our tradition, our culture, our heritage. How can it be denied? It cannot be denied. It is what it was and will always be. With all due respect I ask the Court to find my client Not Guilty." With that he sat down. Tom Mullins would go on to become the next Chief Justice. He was the great orator of the time.

The Court: "Mr. Dannenberg, do you have some closing remarks you want the Court to consider?"

Dannenberg was much more cerebral than Mullins but not as verbally deft. He saw an opening for Gunter Ras, and ran with it.

"Your Honor, I listened intently to the insightful analysis of my colleague. Deferring to his judgment, it is clear to me that based upon the evidence Chairman Warden was simply acting for the safety of the State. Knowing full well her intent, my client was merely following orders. He followed the orders of the Secretary. He believed he was doing what was in the best interest of the State. There can be no crime if there is no criminal intent. Rightly or wrongly he perceived Leslie Marcus as an enemy of the State. If he was mistaken in fact as to her true intentions there is still no evidence of criminal intent. He perceived her as an enemy of the State based on the actions and conduct of the Chairman. He was simply a good soldier in the service of the Chairman. That he was fundamentally mistaken as to Leslie Marcus' status as an enemy combatant is all the more reason to throw the charge of murder out. If anything he might be guilty of a negligent homicide but even that is a stretch. You can't create criminal conduct where there is no criminal intent." With that he rested.

The Chief Justice looked down at the defendants. They were a pathetic lot. Their fall from power had been so sudden and severe that one could only speculate what went through their minds.

He began to address attorney Mullins and the Secretary.

"This Court is appalled by the government sanctioned loss of life in this case. Throughout these proceedings the defendant Warden has been afforded the best counsel the government could provide. She was afforded an opportunity to confront her accusers and to cross-examine them. She was afforded an opportunity to explain her actions and conduct. The Court finds it most interesting that defendant Warden was aware of the existence of the Library, and that she took no steps to provide the benefits of the Library to the greater population. We will never know what her precise knowledge was, but of this the Court is certain. She knew of the writings of Thomas Paine, and believed that her regime was threatened by those writings. There is no other way to explain the callous murder of Leslie Marcus. With regard to the murder of the children, from time immemorial human life has been regarded as sacred. We go to special lengths to preserve animals at the zoo. We even have special sections for the primates. Were these children entitled to less than the animals at the zoo because they failed to meet the yardstick set by the Chairman? The Court thinks not. There is a sacred element to human life that was recognized in the most primitive human societies. To disregard that sacred trust in this day and age is to throw away our heritage and the spiritual nature of mankind. This Court does not accept the defendant's argument that she was only acting to defend the State. This Court finds as a matter of fact that defendant Warden was only acting to preserve her own position of power and that in point of fact, she is guilty beyond a reasonable doubt of the murder of all of the children at Kinder Haus in Buffalo, Kansas and guilty of conspiracy to commit murder and murder in the case of Leslie Marcus. With regard to the case of Gunter Ras his defense that he was only following orders is no defense at all. There is a long human tradition that says every military office is bound to examine the orders given to him, and if they violate his conscious or the perceived mores of society, he is bound to disobey such orders, even at the risk of imprisonment or death. Gunter Ras was more than a mere officer. He was a member of the Inner Circle of the Secretariat. He was charged with a higher duty. He violated his duty as a Legionnaire, as an American and as a human being. The Court finds him guilty of the murder of Leslie Marcus. Sentencing is set for 90 days hence. Court is adjourned. The defendants are remanded to the custody of the Penal Authorities to await sentencing."

Chapter 38

The Sentencing

Tom Mullins would soon learn that the worst thing about a trial was sentencing. There was always an air of uncertainty. If the prosecution had its way every defendant would go to prison or swing by the rope.

Prosecutors were a strange bunch. They got to cherry pick their cases and if they lost it was because of ineptness or prosecutorial misconduct. On the other hand there was the feeling that if the defense won it was not because of the brilliance of counsel. It was either because the prosecution screwed up or the defendant was factually innocent. In any case the defendant's attorney did not deserve any of the credit.

The case had now been submitted for sentencing to the Chief Justice. Tom silently prayed that by some miracle he would spare his client. He recognized the chance was slim, but hope springs eternal.

All of the players were present save the CJ. Tom turned to Dannenberg at his right.

"I really wonder what he is going to do."

Dannenberg was much more pragmatic and not prone to false hope.

"Tom, you don't get it! There are over 400 dead bodies. Someone has to pay. I don't care what the excuses are. There is also something else that lurks just below the surface. This new government has its own agenda. It has to finish off the old regime in a very public way or else it is going to fall on its face. It can't afford to leave sworn enemies alive to confront it down the line. Our clients are not the loyal opposition who share the same beliefs in democratic values that the government exposes. Think about it."

"Yeah, I know. That's what worries me so much. I keep wondering what this trial was all about."

As he was finishing his remark, the Chief Bailiff stood up.

"The Court will come to order. God bless this honorable Court. God bless the United States."

The Chief Justice walked in and sat down. There was silence. He waited for a few moments and then addressed defense counsel.

The Court: "Counsel, is there any legal cause why sentence should not be imposed?"

Tom Mullins: "None that I can think of your honor."

Dannenberg: "No sir."

The Court: "Secretary Warden, the evidence in this case has shown that you are guilty of the crime of mass murder. The explanation offered by you in mitigation of your acts displays a callous indifference to human life. It is the sentence of this Court that you be remanded to the custody of the Prison Authority and at a time set by the Authority be publicly hanged by the neck until you are dead, so that all may see that this government places the highest value on human life and anyone who kills without justification will suffer the severest penalty this Court can impose.

"General Ras, yours was a wanton murder of a young woman. You displayed no remorse for your crime. You gave no mercy to your victim. You silenced Leslie Marcus as if she were simply a barnyard animal to be slaughtered. You are without compassion. It is the sentence of this Court that you be remanded to the custody of the Prison Authority, and at a time set by the Authority be publicly hanged by the neck until you are dead. Your sentence is to be carried out at the same time as that of Defendant Warden. When you are dead this Court is ordering the Prison Authority to burn your bodies and scatter your ashes at a secret location at sea. The location is never to be disclosed for the next 1,000 years. You will not become martyrs to any cause. You are common criminals who are to be excised from the memory of this Country."

The reconstituted judiciary lacked a Court of Appeal. It was in its infancy. It was not a perfect trial. There never is a perfect trial. All of the relevant facts had come out. Sometimes it is better not to know how evil people can be. There was a danger that the sentences would not be carried out. The terrorists had taken up the cause of the Secretary, and threatened to burn the entire Citadel. It was not an idle threat. Gaul took it quite seriously. Terrorism would become part of the pandemic that plagued America for the next 200 years.

Chapter 39

The Emergence of Maribeth Cooper

Gaul was exhausted from the affairs of State. He had destroyed the symbols of the Secretariat. Secretary Warden no longer posed a threat to the Republic. There were pockets of counter revolution throughout the country. His desk was piled high with communications from thousands of people, each asking for some personal favorable treatment. He wanted to throw up from the self indulgent fools. In a few months a Congress of sorts would convene as a unicameral body to chart the course of the country. It would elect a president and Gaul hoped to fade to gray.

"General, here is an interesting note. It seems that this woman wants access to the Library to answer the question, "Why?""

Both men chuckled.

Gaul wondered to himself, "What kind of fool is this one?"

Conversely, sometimes fools should be listened to. He was exhausted, and his patience was at an end. Nation building was too daunting a task for one man. A little amusement would not hurt.

"Lieutenant, take a couple of your men and fetch this woman here!"

"When sir?"

"Now!"

Lieutenant Baker found himself standing outside the door to Maribeth's apartment. Being a direct action kind of a fellow, he banged on the door and elected not to use the ringer. It was Sunday. The affairs of State do not depend on the calendar day.

Maribeth came to the door in due course.

"May I help you, what do you want?"

"You're to come with us. General Gaul has summoned you."

Lieutenant Baker refused to answer any other questions. The truth was he had nary a clue why she was being summoned. He was just carrying out his orders. No matter how many times Maribeth asked, "Why does he want me?" the answer was the same.

"I'm just following orders."

As they walked out to the street, she could hear the sound of his boot click on the hard pavement. There was a cadence to the sound and she felt a tingling fear in her neck and back with each step. She kept wondering, what does Gaul want from me? In her mind she knew that this was not a social call. She had difficulty keeping up with their brisk walk. She feared if she did not they would simply drag her along. Her question kept coursing through her mind. She had no answer. All she could hear in her mind was the clickty-click of their walk.

When they arrived at the General's study Maribeth waited in apprehension for him to enter the room. All about her she saw books. These were the things she had often dreamed of, the icons of the Library. She wanted to reach out and touch one of the books.

Gaul entered the room and immediately asked, "Why do you want access to the Library?"

She was not prepared to answer his question. She was still marveling at the books. Fearful that she had offended the new supreme leader through something she could not recount doing, she wondered if he was about to kill her or order her execution. She could not imagine why, but such things did happen under the rule of the Secretariat. Why should this be any different?

"I always wanted to touch a book. May I touch one of your books?"

Gaul was equally taken aback. What was this strange woman about. "Why do you want to touch a book?"

"Because I always wanted to know why? Perhaps the answer can be found in books. I don't know, but at least the books can answer why to some things."

They began a rapid discussion of where the new government was going. Gaul did not realize they had talked so long. He had found a totally inquiring mind that was not content to merely accept the order of the day, but that questioned the order and the assumptions on which it was based. He was totally fascinated. Where did this creature come from?

"Of course you'll have access to the Library. But tell me something, what do you think of our revolution?"

Maribeth thought for a moment. She wondered to herself, is this the time for complete candor? Without a second thought she launched into her view.

"General, I don't believe your revolution is going to succeed. You have a lot of yes men around you, but no one who asks, why. The teachers in the Kinder Haus do not ask why. If you don't ask why, you will never create a foundation for democratic institutions. It's that simple. Educators have to question the basis of the assumptions they are imparting to kids and adults. It's the questioning process that forms the basis of responsive government. The educators have to be taught to ask "Why?"

She had said all she knew.

A calm feeling came over Gaul. This woman's basic insight would be a key element in the reconstruction of the nation.

"Would you be willing to serve as the National Director of Education?"

A smile came across Meribeth's face. Here she had been certain that something bad was going to happen to her. Now the Director of Education. More could not be asked for in life.v

Chapter 40

The Hanging

In England and early America, executions had been public spectacles. There was great levity. Hucksters sold their wares and street entertainers performed for the enjoyment of the public. As the nation became more sensitive executions were held behind closed doors. An attempt was made to dignify the process and to make it painless for the condemned. Gaul was acutely aware of the history of capital punishment. He also knew that no matter how you viewed an execution, it was nothing more than a State sanctioned homicide. It was entertainment for the on lookers and final for the defendant. It was the ultimate societal ostracism, the final accounting.

Executions are difficult to watch. They are never the sentimental things of movies and love stories.

The Prison Authority built a scaffold. It stood 30 feet above the ground and was constructed of sturdy wood beams. There was a steep stairway leading up to the floor of the scaffold. Two ropes dangled from the upper beam. Each rope was tightly curled around to form a large noose.

The day of reckoning had come. It was a sunny day. There were white wisps of clouds in the sky. The Chairman and Ras were led out into the yard. Bleachers had been set up for the invited spectators. Television cameras covered every inch of the panorama.

The Chairman did not look like her old self. He hair color was splotchy and her hair was ratted in a bun. She seemed to have put on a lot of weight while in prison. Her dress had the appearance of a sack. There was no longer any shape to her body. She had to be helped up the steep stairs. She was a dead woman walking. Her arrogance was gone.

Gunter Ras appeared to be talking to himself. As he sat in the bleachers, attorney Dannenberg wondered if it was proper to execute an insane man. Obviously Gunter had lost whatever sanity he had. Dannenberg had met with him 8 hours before the scheduled execution to see if there was anything else that he wanted him to do. Gunter was completely incoherent.

Tom Mullins had made a last minute personal appeal to Gaul to stay the execution and intervene in the proceedings. Gaul refused to hear him out. His final remark was, "This is a matter for the judiciary. I will not intervene in another branch of government. Even if I wanted to give executive clemency, I would not do so in this case."

There was a conversation taking place between each defendant and the head of the Prison Authority. Dannenberg could not hear it, but perhaps he would see it again on the television in the evening.

The Prison Authority guards pinioned the arms and legs of each defendant. A black bag was placed over their heads and then the noose was cinched tightly about their necks.

The head of the Prison Authority looked at his watch, nodded to another guard and the trap was opened. The defendants fell to their death. They hung there for an hour before being cut down. There was no heartbeat. There was a deep ligature mark around each of their necks. All that was visible of their eyes was the white eyeball. Their faces had a blue pallor of death by strangulation. It was over for now. When they fell there was no applause or outpouring of emotion. Until their fall the crowd had been boisterous. A stifling silence pervaded the bleachers. There were no tears or sighs of regret. There was a certain knowledge that the age of the Secretariat had come to an end. The symbols of the Secretariat had been destroyed.

The crowd in the bleachers slowly exited.

The death of Secretary Warden did not mean the end of terrorism, but at least the Republic had a chance.

Epilogue

In the blackness of the night, Gaul held Jocelyn in his arms. He could not conceive of life without her. She had captured his mind and stolen his soul. He hoped they would have a long life together. For the first time in his life he felt like he was not alone. He longed for a time when he and Jocelyn could retreat from public life and simply enjoy the pleasure of each other. The government was getting stronger. He believed that if you give a man a chance and show him the difference between right and wrong, he will usually try to do the right thing. Sometimes evil people would come along but he would continue to fight for what was just and right. Jocelyn looked at him. He belonged to her and to no one else. She would never let him go.

ABOUT THE AUTHOR

ROSS GALLEN

Ross Gallen was born in New York and raised in California. Growing up during the turbulent Soviet / US nuclear era, he was acutely aware of the lack of civil liberties in the Soviet hegemony. This ingrained a lifelong belief that the Constitution was all that protected ordinary Americans from arbitrary government action. His writing career began as an Op.Ed. writer for his high school newspaper. Graduating from the University of Redlands, he simultaneously received a Bachelor of Science degree in Geology and a Bachelor of Arts in Sociology. After a short stint in graduate school at the University of California, he proceeded to Cal Western Law School where he earned his Juris Doctor Degree.

Ross is a member of the State Bar of California and the State Bar of Texas. Employed as a Deputy District Attorney he argued the landmark case of In re Kay before the California Supreme Court. He honed his skills as a trial lawyer by working as a deputy Public Defender representing clients charged with capital murder and serious felony crimes, and then went on to become a managing partner in a civil litigation firm. He has been a Judge Pro Tem of the Orange County Superior Court and is recognized as a pre-eminent lawyer in the Martindale-Hubbell Bar Register of Pre- eminent Lawyers in America. Ross currently devotes his time to writing fiction and practicing law. Both of his sons are airline pilots and his daughter is a speech pathologist.